Brett J Jenkins is a Western Australian writer and has a PhD from Murdoch University in English and Comparative Literature. He has self-published an autobiography entitled *The Boy Miner: Tales from the Australian Underground* (2019) which tells the story of the four years he worked FIFO before making his shift into studying literature.

THE NOSTALGIA DETECTIVE

BRETT J JENKINS

THE NOSTALGIA DETECTIVE

To my most beautiful son

| 1 |

April 2018: One day after his birthday

I remember these past two weeks like they were a stranger's story overheard at a dinner party, rising above clinking glasses, cutlery scraping on china, low-volume Norah Jones, and the murmurs and squeals of unrelated children playing upstairs. The stranger's story is heard just the once, and its retelling is, at best, a vague and muddled paraphrase, somewhere between absolute truth, and the scandalous improvisation of a tabloid. Which is also to confess that this story is, for the most part, a stranger's, but one that has unavoidably blended with my own.

To add to this foreshadowy tenuousness, I am retelling it, somewhat dramatically, from a hospital bed in Albany, on the southern coast of Western Australia, with a broken lower leg, several cracked ribs, various lacerations and bruises, and the light meandering fog of post-op anaesthesia. It is the morning after the accident. I have a nurse watching over me, sometimes two – a woman and a man. Petal is a South Sudanese-born woman, in her late fifties, and prefers summer to winter. Marcus is in his late twenties, a stoic vegan who occasionally eats fish. They are the captive audience for my story, as they keep a low-key vigil for my very own suicide watch, half-believing the eyewitness accounts that what happened yesterday at the summit of Bluff Knoll (close to one hour from Albany as the crow flies) was no accident and I might just have the hutzpah to have another go. Petal listens, makes me feel heard, brings me back from the figurative cliff edge; and Marcus brings the muscle if Petal's comforting words fail. I have no intention in taking my own life, now or before. I have too much purpose, too much to live for, and a family who needs me. And I have my story to tell which is proof of my desire to carry on. And it distracts me from the pain, especially when the morphine fades, which feels like a lover waving goodbye from a departing train.

My situation affords me time to tell this story. I tell it to them – Petal and Marcus – and write it for you or whoever reads this. Petal says that I am stalling, because I haven't yet phoned Quinn (my wife of fifteen years) who is at home with Maynard (our six-year-old son), some five hours away, in Perth. I haven't called Quinn, but I have messaged her, just this morning in fact – a quick hello and see you soon – but nothing about where I am or what's happened. I will, soon. But let me tell some of it first, to keep her from worrying. And I must also get it down, while it's fresh; before the fabric of the most recent past becomes too old, tattered, and moth-holed to make any sense of it.

Fourteen days until his birthday

It began with an email, which arrived with a muted 'ding' in my inbox as I sat at my desk in the small study on the second floor of our townhouse (rented), overlooking one of the leafy streets of our little suburb just on the outskirts of the Western Suburbs of Perth. The email fell amongst new bill reminders, a notification for an upcoming school assembly, optimistic spam, and several job-seeking emails from my past life that I'd been meaning to unsubscribe from.

Not that long ago, I was a forensic psychologist. Now, I am a stay-at-home dad (my day job), and a casual private detective (my other day job) which is what this particular email pertained to. I had anticipated it, forewarned and forearmed by a former colleague of mine from the force.

Coffee to my lips, blowing off steam, this is how it read:

> Dear Dr Nostalgia,
> Please can you help us. My husband, Richard Curtz, is missing. It's been over six weeks now. I was given your name by Detective Smith. He thinks this is something you could help with, better than what the police can do anyway. Richie is 39 years old, five-eleven. Aquarius. I have attached a recent photo, taken early February.
> Please call me on 04xx xxx xxx.
> We are becoming desperate and you are our only hope.
> Kim.

Our only hope. For a self-lauding moment, I took pleasure in being called upon in the same way that the great jedi Obi wan Kenobi was implored by a low-res holographic Princess Leia. But I wasn't the only hope; I knew there were some good people looking for Richie, even if they were approaching the case from different foci to my own. And this case warranted something different because white, middle-aged, married men do not typically go missing. From the information sent by my colleague prior to the email, I also knew that Richie was upper-middle class (although not always) and heterosexual (seemingly always). You might say that this combination of details renders our Richie unremarkable, near on negligible, invisible – you could hardly see him, even when he was standing right in front of you. Can you see Richie? Can you picture him, in your mind's eye? Yes? No? Certainly, from my neck of the woods,

Perth, Western Australia, you can't see the trees for the forest. He is a dime a dozen, ubiquitous as our summer's sunshine. But this vague description – white, male, middle-class, hetero – also made his disappearance rather enigmatic, atypical. I can say this with confidence because his description is essentially my own, and, in a few months, I will also be turning the big four-o (although, unlike Richie, I am a shade under five-foot-ten and a non-practicing Leo).

The digital photo attached was of Richie and his children – two girls – who looked to be about fourteen and twelve. All three are posed reluctantly, standing at the front of what must be their home. Richie has mousy-brown hair, languishing in the early stages of recession. Pursed lips, weakish chin. Handsome nose. He looked to weigh about 100 kilograms, which was about 10 or 15 heavier than his height and body shape should allow. His was a 'dad-bod' – love handles, paunchy belly, budding man-boobs. He was dressed in a dark-blue suit, red tie, white shirt, all of which sat uncomfortably, a little too tight, as if fitted for a different man. He looked like he *could* afford a better-fitting suit for this chubbier frame but for some reason, possibly vanity or optimism, chose not to. The suit jacket was slung over his shoulder and the dark stains of arm-pit sweat were clear for all to see.

The girls were about two years in age and three inches in height apart, but near identical, and individualised only by their facial expressions, the older brandishing a formidable teen scowl, bunching folds of skin between her eyes and forehead, and the hint of clear braces between an unwilling grimace. The younger sister's eyes were bright, clear, and she wore an excited, toothy smile, which, when contrasted with the elder's, came off as brashly naïve. It looked to be the first day of the school year, from a few months ago, the girls dressed in private-school uniforms, with their boaters and unseasonable ties and jackets. Contrary to their dispositions, the older sister's uniform was fresh-creased and bright whereas the younger's looked to be a hand-me-down, slightly faded, blurry chequers on the dress. Like Richie's suit, this could seem unusual.

Kim is unseen, assumedly orchestrating from behind the camera lens. As is my way, I was both suspicious and cynical: including the children in the photo with Richie was a conspicuous attempt at garnering sympathy from me. Maybe I will take the case if there are kids involved. Maybe I will try a little harder, go the extra mile to get their missing dad home, make their family whole again. Parent to parent. Maybe I will. Heck, of course I will. Besides, I am afforded selectivity with my cases, but, without a doubt, I would take this case, not only for Kim or the children, not only because of Richie's and my similarities, but for something else, which, for storytelling purposes, is better explained later.

I printed the picture out and stuck it on the vacant cork pinboard near my desk, a red thumb tack to match Richie's red tie.

I then sent a text to Kim:

> Hi Kim, I would be happy to consider taking your case. We can meet at Perk-u-late Me, on Mainstreet. 9am, Wednesday (tomorrow), if that suits? Regards, John (Dr Nostalgia).

I wanted to add: 'Perk, like Central Perk in *Friends*'. (I have from a very young age an unhealthy addiction to sitcoms.) But pop culture references aren't for everyone, or at least mine are not necessarily yours.

Kim got back to me immediately, like she was peaking over my shoulder the whole time, intuiting, predicting, already responding as my text was still being carried by wave and wire.

Thank you, Dr Nostalgia. I know the place. Much appreciated, K

Both John and Dr Nostalgia are pseudonyms for when I started moonlighting in the missing persons business. The latter was a nickname graciously given to me by my colleagues when I completed my PhD in forensics. The title and idea for my thesis was a blatant rip-off from Orson Welles' *Citizen Kane*: 'The Rosebud code: Popular culture and the significance of nostalgia in discovering deliberately missing persons.' (There were far worse titles – longwinded, confusing – at the graduation ceremony). Put simply, if we find the missing's pop-cultural 'Rosebud', then we find the missing – deliberately missing people to be specific, those missing by their own volition. It must have sounded interesting to the examiners as it was eventually approved. Just make sure you change the en dashes to em, and Michigan is a state, not a city.

This was the 'doctor' part – the forensic psychology part, of Dr Nostalgia. The 'nostalgia' part was a bit tongue-in-cheek, a pinch of salt to remind me, as much as my clients, that this wasn't always your normal detective work, and 'whodunnit' is most likely the fantasia of the past. This was also the primary 'hunch' of my work: if I find the missing alive, then nostalgia is the abductor. If I find them dead, then nostalgia is the murderer. Or nostalgia is the weapon – not the kind capable of a puncture wound or blunt-force trauma, but more like a paring knife wielded by time, administering death by a thousand cuts. It is all of these, and none.

Maybe 'Dr Nostalgia' is misleading. It's like calling myself Dr Zodiac killer, or Dr Professorplumwiththecandlestickinthestudy. Of course, the first wouldn't attract clients, and the second would hardly fit on a business card.

Detective Smith (also a pseudonym created for this retelling) was the former colleague of mine from the force, and had suggested Kim contact me. Smith was a top detective with a decorated record, having solved several well-known murders and some of the most difficult cold-case missing persons in Western Australia. Thirty-plus years in the force had made him gruff and jaded and, just like a 44-magnum-toting Dirty Harry, was Machiavellian in his convictions. But where others weren't sympathetic to my leaving the force, nor to my unorthodox thesis, Smith had seen the potential of introducing pop culture into the mix. After all, mass murderers and serial killers are the darlings of the pop culture scene. Despite their horrific crimes, Ted Bundy and Charles Manson had more charisma than any Kardashian, not least because, disturbing as it may be, they had a sense of purity and authenticity about their motives, a reality that was attractive to reality-TV audiences, and not just the hardcore devotees and copycats. Docos, biopics always rated well when the worst of us, the most frightening, are given a primetime spot (why else would the Discovery Channel dedicate a whole week to sharks). Smith also trusted my gut instinct, even if he didn't always agree with me, and even when he was worried our association could cost him a bit of his cop-credibility. Which is why we kept it clandestine, with him surreptitiously passing cases on to me, including all the backstories, photos, and evidence to keep me up to speed. I was working with no clear jurisdiction, with few resources and even fewer allies.

Thirteen days until his birthday: Meeting with Kim; John Doe

I was tired the morning following the email, having stayed up too late reading over Richie's file. When I did finally get to bed, it was a disturbed sleep, my mind continuing to trawl over the details, working through the few facts I knew and those I expected to find. I could have easily slept another hour or two, a symptom also of the beginning of autumn, that peculiar liminal time of the year where the new season hasn't really kicked in but the days are growing shorter, which comes unexpectedly, habitualised to the long hot days, barbecues at seven in the evening, Maynard bouncing on the trampoline until eight, me peeling a sweaty shirt off my back most of the day. Then, suddenly, the sun starts to come at you from different angles, it drops earlier and stays away longer, as it falls quickly away from the flattest part of its ellipse. There was general confusion about the house, starting dinners earlier, waking up later, rushing to get ready for school, the washed clothes no longer drying within minutes of being on the line.

Quinn was in the shower and Maynard was standing uncannily near our bed, watching me as I fingered crusted sleep from my eyes.

'Daddy, I'm hungry. Can I have my cornflakes, please?' he said as he scratched at his straw hair, my immediate thought being that head lice had set up shop.

'Of course. It's late, isn't it? I'll bet you're hungry. Big or small bowl?'

'Big bowl.'

'A big bowl for a big boy.' Maynard loved it when I called him a big boy, which he took to be an indisputable fact despite being both short in stature and slight in frame. And he would most times eagerly run over to the doorway marked with pencil scratches and dates to show his growth and time passing, where he would hand-measure himself inaccurately to see how much he had sprouted. An inch taller, maybe two, in a day, no less! Inspired, he would run to the bathroom and look in the mirror to see if his new front teeth were coming in. Other kids his age had been losing their milk teeth, and it happens at different times for every child, but Maynard had lost his early from a fall on a climbing frame, knocking the two front teeth out. It was a horrific trauma in itself, the long hours in the hospital waiting room, an operation to clear the remnant teeth fragments. But the tragedy lay not only in his cherubim face being disfigured by the gummy gaping maw, but in its prematurity, the gummy gaping maw having come too early, aging him by a year or two in a slip in time, depriving us of a most precious period of his childhood that was already getting away from us. We are selfish with our time, stingy in letting it pass, downright inconsolable when it is stolen.

He would relive this same moment every morning, this drama of looking for new teeth, and I would pause, waiting for him to return to the kitchen table, and attempt to ease his disheartened mind at finding the same desolate gums.

'Soon, buddy. You'll get them soon.'

'Okay.' It was a word that slumped, along with the little slumping shoulders of a six-year-old for whom there was nothing more pressing than getting bigger, getting older, growing teeth. He might not have recognised it but he was getting older, in his body, but more so in his mind which was overflowing with new and complex desires and emotions, bringing with it an increased sense of self and the nature of his existence, the reality of himself.

I poured crisp Corn Flakes into his bowl, added the milk and set him up at the table, where he began intently shovelling, every trouble temporarily forgotten.

As he ate, I made myself a coffee which gave me the kick I desperately needed. 'Remember when Corn Flakes was pretty much the only choice for breakfast,' I said to Quinn (now out of the shower) as she pinballed around the kitchen preparing to head off to work. 'That and Weet-bix. I swear muesli wasn't even invented when I was a kid.'

'Uh huh,' she replied, indifferently, permissible in our well-seasoned relationship, dismissing the disruption to her routine with the trivialities of the past, gently swatting it away like the tedious fly that it was.

Quinn is a clinical psychologist, top notch as far as I can tell, spending her very expensive billable time trying to get clients to overcome their childhood traumas, their fractured relationships with their parents, and their very specific PTSD. She is like a beat cop trying to move on loiterers, rubberneckers, fascinated by the blood and bodies of a car accident; except, in this analogy, Quinn's patients are both the victims and the onlookers, looking for explanations, not treatment, fascinated by their own open wounds, wondering of their cause, unsure of how their emotionally rough-running vehicle ended up on its roof.

'They add more breakfast choices but take away the permeate from our milk and the gluten from our bread and cereal,' I continued. 'Maybe I *want* my permeate; maybe I *want* my gluten'.

'For your information, *Seinfeld*, gluten has been making people sick for decades.' She was listening after all, sorting through the bullshit, the most crucial skill of her – our – profession. I was forensic, she was clinical. Uni sweethearts. Her career was taking off just as I was questioning mine. I needed a break: ten years in the force wearies the soul, or hardens it, or breaks it. Most metaphors around detriment, decay and destruction will do. There's only so many stories of child abuse, spousal abuse, murder, torture, that the emotional sacrificial anode of the soul can take. I hadn't realised that, under the façade of 'work' was a crippling accumulation of grief, anger, and fear. Which is why when Maynard was born (healthy if not a little undersize – not quite a fish to be thrown back) I took leave to become a stay-at-home dad. From hard-boiled detective to a gooey, runny yolk of a home-husband.

Thus, my routine:

Cornflakes.

Theatre of teeth.

Make school lunch.

Get dressed.

Off to school.

And then the day was mine, to cook and clean and find missing persons.

I dropped Maynard at school, chatted briefly with fellow mums and dads, before making my way to Perk-u-late Me. Perk was the local coffee shop, just a block away from the school, and two blocks from our home. The coffee is good enough, which convenience made up for. I asked Kim to meet me there because I have no dedicated office other than the study at home which doubles as a storeroom for old baby stuff, suitcases, unused electronic gizmos, and trebles as a second playroom with tubs of Lego, a cache of toy weapons, and dress-up costumes. Another reason for a public meeting was to keep my various lives separate from theirs. It is an inevitable occupational hazard that I will become ingrained in my clients' lives: like any psychologist, they will tell me the most intimate details about themselves, reveal things no one else knows, some they would happily have taken to the grave with them; and confidentiality, crypt-like, is a professional expectation, theirs and mine. And sometimes they want me to go further in the investigation, seeing me almost like a conduit or medium between them and their missing. I don't necessarily bring the missing back – there are no guarantees that I will deliver them to their loved ones' door – I just locate them, show the families where their missing are. There's not much more that can be done after that. It's easy to forget that the missing are missing *only* because they are missed. This means that the missing aren't always lost and have in fact chosen to be missing, as free individuals – in some ways more free than any of us. If they want to come home, they will. If they want to stay missing, then they are free to do that too.

I arrived on time at the café. Kim wasn't there yet. I knew what she looked like from her business website, part of the research that had kept me up the previous night. She was a Personal Trainer, with a background in physiotherapy. Her business was simply called 'Kim's fitness' with the tagline 'A fit future is in your hands.' A bit of an alliterative mouthful but got the message across.

I ordered a hot flat white, grabbed the store copy of the newspaper, and took a seat inside amongst the hearty din of the post-school-drop-off crowd. The paper's headline – a refrain from the last month or so – was about the Claremont Serial Killer trial, which Smith had been integral in uncovering. There was little in the story that I hadn't already been privy to and, in need of something lighter, flicked past the local and global troubles towards the middle where the funnies and puzzles were: Calvin was tobogganing and philosophising with Hobbes; Cathy was fighting the good fight; and Modesty Blaise was very erotic but offered little in the way of closure. The quick crossword was filled and the cryptic crossword was complete bar one word. The final clue: 'Look ashore! A bubbly enemy to Mary.' One word, seven letters; second letter an *e*; second last letter an *a*. I assumed that both the *e* and *a* were correct, given that the cross word with the *a* was *aqua* and the *e* came from *shame* and the rest of the crossword seemed to fit neatly in the chequered grid. Of course, the *e* could be impersonating an *a*; and the scrawled *a* could just as easily be mistaken for an *o*.

Engrossed as I was, I missed Kim walking in, not until she was standing right in front of me. She was wearing an iteration of the Western Suburbs school mum's athleticwear look: black Nike long-sleeve top, worn under a black North Face puffer vest, sleek metallic finish on the leggings, looking like a sexy cyborg fish, with a tight blonde ponytail sticking out the back of her black Nike hat, between the little hole made by the strap. That and her mirrored aviator sunglasses made her look just like Linda Hamilton's Sara Conner from *Terminator 2*, cut and buff from her time in the Pescadero State Hospital for the Criminally Insane, and all geared up with her assault rifle and fatigues to take on the T1000. Unlike the more weathered Sara Conner of *T2*, Kim maybe had some fillers in her lips, Botox in the creases around her mouth and brow. Either she was trying to wind back the clock, or just doing her best to slow the inevitable, which adhered to her 'A fit future is in your hands/ No fate but what we make' mantra. And instead of an assault rifle under her arm, she carried a shoe box.

She spotted me just as easily, having told her I'd have with me a brown fedora – a gift from Quinn when I first made detective, harking back to either Bogey's Marlowe, from *The Big Sleep* or, Bogey's Sam Spade from *The Maltese Falcon*. She found it at a Salvos, likely donated by the recently-bereaved of the recently-deceased. It was well used, ragged and scuffed where fingers from the past have clutched at it, or doffed and tipped, gentleman-like. Quinn thought it hilarious – a cute joke, made at my expense. But for a week I wore it non-stop – school drop-offs, food shopping, a dinner party – until she conceded that it had backfired spectacularly. Now I carry it only as a prop, an affectation, for drawing narrow attention to myself.

Kim sat without ordering, and placed the shoe box (Converse Allstars, high-top, black, size 12) on the table. Up close, her sunglasses now removed and hung on her flak-jacket vest, she looked tired, wore no makeup, and had a burning question on her unglossed lips: 'Can you help us?'

For her sake, I should have hesitated. 'Yes, I think so.'

'Sorry for being so blunt but I don't have the patience for any more niceties or friendly introductions. I have met so many people: police, detectives, friends come to help, neighbours bringing cakes and quiches. Everyone. We have money. Enough to pay whatever is necessary.'

Her voice broke with fatigue and uncertainty and she was ready to cry, unwilling to look me in the eye, wiping at her mouth to hide a trembling chin. She looked guilty, not of murder (one possibility for his disappearance), but of some form of irresponsibility – a neglectful wife that has misplaced her husband.

'Bluntness is understandable, given the difficult circumstances,' I said, offering a smile that might normally be reserved for funerals, tax audits. 'Yes, I can help. But if I can also be blunt, what makes you think he is missing, you know, missing missing, in the common sense of the word, and hasn't just . . . left . . . you?'

Kim didn't look affronted by the unflattering question. Likely it had been asked many times over the month since Richie's disappearance and, I suspected, with far less sensitivity. 'Because he hasn't used any of his credit cards and hasn't withdrawn anything from our accounts. How is he living with no money? And as far as I can tell he hasn't taken a single thing with him – no wallet, phone, just the clothes he was wearing. And because Richie wasn't like that. He wouldn't just get up and leave me, and he definitely wouldn't leave the girls. He loves us. And he isn't dead. I can feel it. He's around. He's close. I have a bit of the psychic in me too, you know?'

'Oh, I'm not a psychic,' I said a little too emphatically, and for no good reason added, 'But I don't think he is dead either. What do you last remember?'

Both my confidence in his wellbeing and my question seemed to bring a glint of excitement to her eye. 'What I remember most – and this will sound strange – was the smell of mothballs. It was coming from his t-shirt, a band t-shirt, Temple of the Dog, I think. Do you know it?'

'Temple of the Dog? I don't think so.'

'Let me find a picture.' She tapped away at her phone before holding the screen up for me to see. The image wasn't of Richie wearing the t-shirt but came from a webpage that sold various printed tees, modelled by a boy in his late teens wearing a Temple of the Dog self-titled album cover t-shirt. It wasn't anything like the usual band merch sold from a caravan parked outside a concert – this was 100% cotton, and fitted like a luxury brand, with tapered arms to make the biceps look bigger. The boy had expensive-looking dreadlocks too, crafted by an artisan, not from bohemian neglect, and perfectly-manicured eyebrows. Underneath the image of the boy, it read 'You may also be interested in . . .' and had more images of the same model wearing tees with album covers from 'similar' bands: Black Sabbath, The Ramones, Led Zeppelin, The Beatles. For each picture, the boy wore the same bored facial expression fixed to his clean, tanned face as he indifferently travelled backwards through time.

'Does this mean anything?' Kim asked, studying my face.

'Hmm, hard to say.' At this stage it was prudent to be cagey.

'The t-shirt was really creased because he had it stored in a box in the attic, which was also why there was the stink of mothballs. It was really tight on him, around his stomach. He isn't as fit as he used to be. He had his old blue flannelette shirt on too, unbuttoned so that you could see the shirt and because he couldn't button it up. And he was wearing his grey jeans, with holes in the knees. The denim was thin at the crotch and had a hole, so I told him to fix them up or throw them out. Can you believe he dug out my mother's old sewing machine, jumped on YouTube for instructions on how to use it and sewed them up himself. Such a stubborn prick.' She smiled absently, with some difficulty, as if pained, like it was the first in months. She then tapped a rough-manicured finger on the shoe box. 'And he was wearing his Converse Allstars, his favourites. He wore them everywhere except at work. I made him keep them outside because of their atrocious stink. Canvas isn't a good material for shoes.

'It was all so strange, which is why it was all so clear to me. I thought he was trying the jeans and t-shirt on for his fortieth birthday party, which is in just over two-and-a-half weeks' time. The theme was my suggestion: "Come as you were" – you know, from the Nirvana song. I didn't think he was looking forward to it, but, all of a sudden, he was wearing his costume. He was still in it when he left for a walk, sometime after dinner, Tuesday night, six weeks ago. That was the last time we saw him.' Kim was trying and failing to temper her enthusiasm as she spoke of the party, of dress-ups, but also of the mystery of it all. 'I was going to wear an old pair of "happy pants" from the op shop, Fluro headband and an old Hypercolour t-shirt I found deep, deep, deep in my closet. I also had a pair of LA Gear hi-tops which I ordered from E-bay. Don't ask how much they cost me.'

'It's in the vault,' I said, dragging an imaginary zip across my mouth. 'Do you have any more photos, closeups? Videos?'

Her excitedness faded, buzz-killed, as she slid the shoe box towards me. 'There's these and I can share the digital folders with you from the Cloud. I also have some home videos.'

'Perfect. I will need everything you've got, as far back as you can go. I also need contact details of close friends, family. Work contacts. Everything. What about his family? Any brothers or sisters?'

'No brothers or sisters. His mother passed away a few years back. She died from melanoma. And his father is in a home down in Mandurah.'

As I jotted these details down in my Moleskin notepad (another affectation) I could feel Kim's eyes on me. 'Detective Smith said that you used to be his partner. What happened? Anything I should know about?'

'Nope, it's all pretty simple, really. I took some paternity leave as we — my wife and I — were having a baby, a boy, and I ended up extending my leave indefinitely.'

'You are so lucky.'

'Yes, I guess I am.'

'To have a boy, I mean. They seem much simpler, less stress.'

'Right. We will see.'

'Take it from me, teenage and tweenage girls are tough. I should know, having once been one if you can believe it.'

'I was once young too,' I said, casting a sympathetic smile.

'Where do we go from here? When can you get started?'

'Right away. But there's also no real rush. I am certain he is safe.'

Kim thanked me but hardly looked reassured as she left the café. Which had to do. And besides, there was no benefit in telling her the hard-to-swallow truth that the missing almost never come back, at least not in the way we like to remember them.

During our conversation, I knew for certain that Kim had lied to me at least three times: the first was by omission, the second an outright untruth, and the third was her unwitting denial of a suspicion held by Smith. The omission was that their house was in turmoil: Richie had been in some recent legal trouble, with a corruption inquiry underway at his accounting firm and the heat was being applied from a number of interested parties including the ATO and the CCC. This was information Smith had given me and was the most plausible reason for Richie taking flight. But Smith didn't think it quite added up. As Kim had said, Richie hadn't drawn any big amounts of money from any of his accounts and he disappeared before the fraud had even been discovered. This was one story. The other was that Richie had been found out by Austin, his business partner, and Austin had made Richie disappear, some way or another, to absolve himself of any connection. And yet another was that Austin was the fraudster and was framing Richie up to take the fall. Richie had found out about it and, knowing he wouldn't be able to prove otherwise (or that he was in danger if he tried), had fled the scene, saving himself, whilst abandoning his family who were now very vulnerable.

The second lie told by Kim (this one blatant and to my face) was that they had money. I knew very well that their finances were in a holding pattern because of the alleged fraud she had only just neglected to disclose. They could pay me something, but I wasn't going to book a family vacay to the Bahamas, or mail the private school application off just yet.

The third – her unwitting denial – was Smith's suspicion of infidelity. This came from his notes, written in the margin by hand. It simply read: 'Affair? Austin?' Maybe a threat to his manhood had caused Richie to leave. Maybe it was a final justification to extricate himself from a marriage that had run its course. At this stage everything was on the table.

Which is a good time to admit that I too had lied to Kim – twice in fact. The first was that I was indeed very familiar with the band Temple of the Dog. Their lineup was a who's who of Seattle's nascent grunge scene: Chris Cornell and Matt Cameron from Soundgarden; and Stone Gossard, Jeff Ament, Mike McCready and

Eddie Vedder who were most of Pearl Jam. They only released the one self-titled album in 1990. If Richie's and my similar demographics had initially drawn me to the case, then this detail had really got me hooked.

It also precipitated my second lie to Kim which was that the t-shirt was without a doubt an important clue. Music, popular music, to be specific, is quintessentially connected to nostalgia and is therefore, as my research argued, connected to the missing. There was one chapter from my thesis, for my mind the most important, that focused on music's nostalgic influence, with two well-trodden quotes for epigraphs: Dick Clark: 'Music is the soundtrack of our lives'; and Aristotle: 'Give me a child until he is seven and I will show you the man.' There is wisdom to be drawn from both these great thinkers: 'Show me the song and I will show you the person,' or, maybe, 'Show me the CD collection and I will find you your missing.' Admittedly, I had long felt there was a possible contradiction in this logic, which defies the direction of influence. Oftentimes, the music we choose to play reflects our mood, or enhances it. If you are feeling heartbroken, then you listen to songs about heartbreak (Sinead O'Connor's cover of Prince's 'Nothing Compares to you' comes to mind). If you are angry, you put on some heavy metal – Metallica, Pantera, maybe some nu metal like Korn, Slipknot or the Deftones – and drive nowhere really fast. But music can also determine our mood. It's what makes us move, gets us up on the dance floor, even if we have no desire to. We tap our feet, nod our heads to beats, part of our evolution and the desire for the reassurance of our mother's heart. The benignity of church is made sublime by the choir, swells the heart. Our bodies' reactions to music tells us how to feel, how to think. Some bands – from Judas Priest to Slayer – are accused of encouraging their fans to suicide or murder, as if it were out of the listeners' hands, shifting blame and responsibility. Not only because of the lyrics, but the combination of words and music, their marriage which affects us so. Who are we? The soundtrack tells us, unfolds our essences for us. And if life was a soundtrack telling us who we are, if our emotions were a jukebox on shuffle, would we not each be sitting on the edge of our seats, leaning forward in anticipation for what song would be played next?

Woodstock had been the case study for the thesis chapter, but I could easily have chosen Depression/prohibition-era Jazz, the eighties and glam rock, New Wave, or the nineties grunge of Richie's and my generation, Generation X. And it is the music of Gen X that had me entertaining an even more significant connection between Temple of the Dog and Richie's disappearance: Chris Cornell, lead singer of Temple of the Dog and Soundgarden had died less than a year ago, taking his own life, suicide by hanging. He was one of the last of the many suicides and deaths via misadventure from the grunge era, almost all of them kids born in the mid-to-late '60s. Kurt Cobain's death was the most recognised, a 'where were you when,' kind of moment. I remember it very clearly: I was turning 16, watching TV at home. It was one of the first stories on the six o'clock news, footage from the 'Smells like Teen Spirit' music video and MTV's Unplugged. His dirty longish-blonde hair, and a fluffy sickly-green cardigan, looking small, like a child dressed in his dad's clothes. I felt this sharp pain of sadness, like 'Oh no, not yet, not now.' It was too soon. I wasn't ready. And yet, amidst the mourning, was exultation, apotheosis. A recognition of it being the most profound, most transformative moment of my young life – even if it was one that began with a suicide.

What this told me – the Temple of the Dog t-shirt, the death of Chris Cornell, and Richie's upcoming fortieth birthday – was that Richie's disappearance was not simply an absconsion, Christopher Skase-like, from a potential fraud and corruption charge, or a fleeing from a flailing marriage, but possibly the outcome of an emotionally-confused midlife crisis, set in motion by the death of a musical icon. Why then did I not tell Kim that the Temple of the Dog t-shirt wasn't an important clue? Maybe because it sounds ludicrous. Or maybe not to elevate her hopes. Or maybe just the opposite.

Petal, my ever-vigilant nurse, has become increasingly perturbed. Until now, she has been listening, intently enough, to my exposition, nodding when she understands, or agrees with something I've said. Her hands twitch occasionally, as if she were used to having knitting needles crisscrossing in her lap. But right now, she is gesticulating in frustration, shaking her head, her mind already made up, not feeling sorry or sympathetic for the man I am looking for.

'So typical of a man to run away scared from getting old. Us, women, are always getting old, and everything and everyone keeps telling us so. You want to feel old? Try menopause. It robs you of your youth and your womanhood. But a man won't understand that, even if they are going bald and fat.'

I thank her for her critical input and look to Marcus, the young male nurse, sitting quietly in the corner, out of Petal's line of sight, who holds his hands up, palms towards me, fingers pointing to the ceiling in a gesture of surrender, one that says, 'I am your white, male comrade, but I ain't touching that.'

'Shall I continue?' I say to Petal, an entreaty of sorts, and an acknowledgement that she has been heard.

She speaks calmly having remembered why she was posted at my bedside to begin with: 'Well, I've got nowhere to be except for watching over you, and I did like hearing about your son. Talk a bit more about him.'

'I will, but in good time.'

'Hmph.'

My meeting with Kim left me feeling enthusiastic and, when I returned home from Perk, I immediately went upstairs to find my boxes of CDs. They took some looking for, having been packed up and stored away around five years ago, from when an infant Maynard, newly mobile, took to pulling them apart, frisbeeing the disks across the room and tainting the covers with peanut butter and watermelon fingers. I couldn't bear it, recalling how my teenage self had treated them so carefully, sacredly, hours and hours spent poring over the inner sleeves deciphering the artwork that sat alongside the lyrics, learning the band members' names, the instruments they played, the brands of the instruments, the other bands they thanked for their support. Until Maynard, nothing in my life had been more precious.

I brought what I could down, and like a child at a toybox, began pawing through them, looking for the Temple of the Dog album, sure that I'd purchased it a few years after its release. Temple of the Dog were like a grungy twenty-somethings' version of the Travelling Wilburys, except Temple were running the wrong way, only just beginning their epoch-defining careers. Despite their pedigree, I remember struggling to get past the first song 'Say Hello to Heaven' which was far too bluesy for me at the time. Granted, the band was mourning the death of Andrew Wood, with the album being their tribute to his passing. But I wanted speed, heavier drums, electric riffs. I wanted music that matched my rising testosterone and aggression levels, a desire that would be better satisfied by the albums that Temple of the Dog's band members would come to produce in their next projects. This also explained why I couldn't find it, a vague recollection of having lent it to a friend and never asking for it back. No matter. I jumped on YouTube where I found several videos of the album in full, some with the original music videos and some with the lyrics, all of them the equivalent of a modern bootleg. I chose the clip with the scrolling lyrics and ran the sound from my computer to our long-forgotten stereo which was coated in sticky dust and tethered to the sideboard by daddy-long-legs webs – a victim of my negligent housework. Even without the dust and cobwebs, it was quite possible that the stereo hadn't been used since bringing Maynard home for the first time from King Edward hospital. Our family home had become a monastery, where peace, and quiet, and white-noise apps took precedence over rock and roll. But with the house to myself, and the past at my finger-tips, I threw care to the wind, wound up the volume to about seven, and clicked the digital 'play' icon. What rose from nothing was the unmistakable jangly hook of Stone Gossard's guitar, Matt Cameron's drums, and then the inimitable Chris Cornell sang. Just as I remembered, it was slow and dark, but this remembering was already being reconstructed, revised, and a sudden vibrancy over-took the house, like every thing within it – furniture, the TV, pot plants, books, *objets d'art* – had become tuning forks, all of them, reverberations, echoes, resonances, and within me, too, a quake of intense joy, a euphoric feeling that I had discovered something new, something appreciated, returning as an echo. There was something else too, which felt far less joyous, instead giving rise to a queasiness in my belly, a weight on my chest. A sickness which felt like regret and loathing, and a longing, ebbing and flowing in the background, intermingling, interfering with my euphoria. This was nostalgia: this mixture of joy and sickness and was undoubtedly a mainline connection to Richie's disappearance.

I kept listening, and began sorting through the Allstars shoebox Kim had given me. It was filled with photos in the protective enve-lopes of mostly-defunct photo marts – Kodak, Pixie. Between the envelopes were loose photos and polaroids. Most were of Richie, with very few taken by him. The camera's eye was his parents' or his friends' and he'd inherited the photos, or they were doubles. They weren't organised in any obvious way, so I pulled them all out, and attempted to find a timeline, from birth, to toddler, to child, to tween, to teenager, to man, to missing.

From the time of his birth, there were only a few grainy yellowing baby photos. In some of these, his heavily-bearded father is holding him. His father is comfortable in the way he bears the boy in his arms. He is also proud, unashamedly smitten. There are some of baby Richie in a sink for a bath, naked, bald penis on display, which, without a doubt, would have featured at his twenty-first birthday, and the comments would have come thick and fast: 'Not much bigger these days, eh Richie?'; 'Jeezus mate, always the bloody exhibitionist!'

Fast forward a few years, late 1970s/early '80s, Richie at a beach, maybe he is two, with one of his grandmothers. Other photos from Christmas with teddy bears, and matchbox cars. At five he has a cast on his arm. His mother in the photo looks tired and concerned beneath a voluminous perm. I imagine his father (like I imagine all fathers of the time) is grinning behind the lens, and talking the usual machoism about character building and being good for him and learning important life lessons etc. etc.

More photos and Richie grows older, loses his baby fat, becomes skinnier, taller. New bikes, footballs, Lego for birthdays. Holiday pics from Darwin and Sydney. He is alone in most of the photos, or with one of his parents, rarely both.

Shots of a farm, assumedly his childhood home, him on a green Kawasaki motorbike; in the background, pastures of the same colour. In other photos, without the bike, some without him, there are dead-wheat brown pastures, farmhouses, sheds. He turns fourteen or so and the pictures become sparser. He is taller yet, approaching his full height, an almost-even six-footer, and there are rashes of pimples and 'wedge' haircuts, baby-toothed-smiles replaced by embarrassed brace-meshed grimaces. His hair gets longer. He stays thin in his neck and shallow in his cheeks. A bum-fluff moustache heralds the onset of puberty, before confirming its place with a thick goatee, high fashion at the time and perfect for veiling a chin like his. He could be good looking, but still he grows ugly, but only relatively, when held up alongside the baby photos. Almost every baby's future is ugly, smelly, hairy, snarky, which is why nature works in slow-motion; otherwise we might not even recognise them, day-to-day, let alone keep them.

Then a photo of him with a metal frame around his head – a broken neck – and a picture of his Kawasaki with the forks buckled in half. Kim said there were VCR tapes of him riding the Manjimup 15000 – a motocross event, running since 1980 – but the neck injury seemed to call this to a halt. And then he is 17 and he is at a graduation, at Scotch College, in Perth. There is a school ball, a mixer with one of the private girls' schools. He wears a hired suit, bow tie, and has his arm around a tall girl in a pink ballgown, a wall of fringe fronting her long dark hair.

And then he is 18 or older and appears only within crowds of friends of which he seems to have many. He is popular and loved. There are a few recurring faces, long hair, facial hair, more flannos, surf t-shirts, jeans; the girls, pre-mid-riffed-Britney, are dressed heavily, covered up, the country friends. But there are other groups of friends too, the Scotch friends, with whom he looks just as comfortable.

One photo stood out from the rest. It was from his eighteenth birthday, back at the farm. He is dancing, frozen mid-dance, drunk or high or both. His eyes are closed, and he is smiling. He is alone in the picture, except for a girl, about the same age, sitting on a low wall nearby. She is off to the side, just out of focus but you can tell her eyes are fastened on him, and she is smiling too. She is not his girlfriend, they are not together, but you could guess that she is in love with him. Or, like so many teenage relationships, she is in love with the idea of him; or she is in love with the idea of love.

Having arranged the photos, I thought to organise my CDs into columns, arranged by year, into what looked like a collaged bar graph of my musical autobiography, and ran them alongside the approximated timeline of Richie's photos. There was a clear rise in the number of albums I owned which mirrored the fall in the number of photos of Richie. The baby photos overwhelmed the late '70s and most of the '80s, whereas the music of the '90s over-whelmed the dwindling documentation of his teen years. It was the music, not photos, that kept the definitive record of who he was, the soundtrack of our lives.

The Temple of the Dog album came to its end. YouTube recommended more albums from the '90s just as the website with the dreadlocked boy had recommended t-shirts. Most of them were already in my bar graph and I chose Soundgarden's *Badmotorfinger* from 1991 and then promised myself that Pearl Jam's *Ten* (also from 1991) would be next. In the same year, Nirvana released *Nevermind*, which ultimately made 'grunge' mainstream. There were other big albums that year too: Metallica's *Black* album, REM's *Out of Time*, and the Chilli Peppers' *Blood Sugar Sex Magik* added to the fantastic artistic milieu that would rarely if ever be repeated. Guns 'n Roses also brought out *Use Your Illusion* 1 and 2 which, despite being hugely popular, would be one of the last of its kind, with glam metal, hair metal, and cock rock, yielding to the grunge takeover. Overnight, bands like Twisted Sister, Poison, Def Leppard, Warrant, Motely Crue, Van Halen, Skid Row, and Bon Jovi suddenly looked very stale, camp, or just plain silly. The unabashed and blatant pursuit of partying and getting laid was out; cynicism and suicide was in.

'Seafoam.' Petal has waited politely for a pause; or the recurring theme of suicide has prompted her to interrupt.

'Sorry?'

'I like cryptic crosswords too. "Look ashore! A bubbly enemy to Mary." That was the clue, wasn't it? Seafoam. If "aqua" and "shame" are correct, then seafoam fits.'

'Amazing.'

'What, you didn't expect a nurse was capable?'

Marcus has left the room.

'All apologies, but I try never to expect anything.'

'That may be so, but I am expecting a doctor soon, to give you an update on that leg of yours. In the meantime, drink some more of your water. Please.'

I packed away the photos and CDs, before making myself lunch, marinating some chicken wings for dinner, and giving the house a quick tidy. By then it was time to pick Maynard up from school. This is a neat way of confessing another lie – a half-truth, really – that I told Kim at Perk, on how I came to be the Nostalgia Detective. It *was* to take paternal leave – this much is true. But the real reason I didn't go back to criminal detecting was because, put simply, I had lost my nerve, for what was a second time.

This needs some explanation. In my earlier days, at high school, I hadn't amounted to much – mediocre grades and an attitude to match. It was much the same after graduation. Truth be told I could have done almost anything, had I set my mind to it, but the freedom of opportunity and the vertigo of an untold future made it impossible for me to decide one way or another. Smart enough to go to university, not driven enough to want any path in particular.

Sick of having me at home, stinking up the lounge, watching shitty daytime TV, and emptying her pantry with bored teen hunger, my mother clipped an ad from the Western Australian newspaper looking for recruits for the police. I applied, passed the physical and psych evaluation, graduated. It seemed promising, but a few months in I realised that, despite the thorough preparation and training for the fieldwork, I was no hero and was not at home on the frontline. Turns out, in fact, that I was, without sugar-coating it, a yellow-bellied coward who was scared of being shot, scared of carrying a gun, and utterly fearful for my own life. Which is why I only did a few years as an officer before quitting. From there, I took a detour into studying forensics. Eight years later, I completed my PhD before returning to the force, this time to the detective side, working behind the scenes, once all the dangerous stuff was taken care of. (If this sounds unconvincing, then so be it. Chances are there are stranger things to come).

Now older and more mature, I grew into my role, was hardened by the experience of studying the behaviour of criminals, psychopaths and sociopaths. I interviewed, probed, and gutted them, working them out, turning them inside out, sifting through the evidence of their lives, disentangling the truth from fiction, scrutinising facial expressions, hand gestures, tics and tells, observing them as they tried their best to look like they are telling the truth. Them knowing that I know they are trying to look like they are telling the truth. And they did tell me things. They confessed not only to their worst crimes, but to who they were. I learned that very few enjoyed enacting violence on others, declaring that it was passion or emotion that drove them to do it. And now the passion had subsided, leaving them with long days of monotonous remorse, bookended by the red-shamed dawn that they woke to each day and the hopeful absolution of the coming nightfall.

Others, far fewer, were at ease with who they woke to – the psychopaths and sociopaths – those puzzled by the hearts and minds of the humans they find themselves living amongst. Indifferent to the pain of others; worse yet, unwilling to try to understand the pain.

If you could see my dreams, better, come to the place of my nightmares, then you would find one of my psychopaths, John Doe, haunting me still. This despite knowing that, within weeks of beginning his lifetime prison sentence, he was killed by a fellow inmate, as is often the case, the security overtly lax. Shivved with a sharpened toothbrush, twenty or more puncture wounds in the chest, which suggested it was done with some enthusiasm. He was dead – an unclaimed bag of cremated ashes – but I couldn't help bringing that dreaming fear back into the real world.

This John Doe had committed an infanticide, which for months leading up to his confession had me in a perennial state of anxiety, as the whole case took place not long after Maynard was born. I was a semi-functioning wreck. I couldn't eat and when I did I had constant nerve-induced diarrhea. There were perpetual ebbing headaches, the shallow breathing of panic attacks. We didn't four-wheel drive, but I convinced Quinn we needed a Landcruiser when driving with Maynard, its height and bulk and bull-bar compensating for my fear. To the dismay of both mine and Quinn's parents, I was reluctant to leave Maynard with them, distrustful of anyone looking after this baby of ours, irreplaceable like nothing else in the world is irreplaceable. This child, utterly defenceless and unaware that he needs protection against this world in which police and detectives try to maintain the semblance of peace. But the thin blue line isn't a line like an equator dividing the world into two halves of good and evil. The thin blue line is no line at all. It is a fragile space that can be assailed at any angle, at any time, by anyone, with your eyes open or your back turned. And amidst this chaos was our perfect baby

Maynard, dribbling and shitting and pissing and smiling obliviously to all that was harmful and hurtful in the world.

All my fears culminated in the last interview with John Doe – last because, after a long and drawn-out search and interrogation, he did us a favour and finally confessed. I remember it vividly. He was sat across from me and Smith at a plain Formica table, him cuffed, in the sickly fluorescent-lit interrogation room of the station. It was a horrible room: rough-cleaned, bleach in the air, walls plain, as if to sterilise it, drain it of stimulus; so different to the one in which Roger 'Verbal' Kint, played by Kevin Spacey, finds himself in during his interrogation in *The Usual Suspects*. Unlike Verbal, my man had nothing but the canvas of whitewashed walls to paint what was in his mind. He had a steel face, from the blue stubble on his jaw, silver hair on the sides of his tonsured head, and eyes that shone like dime-mirrors. He was ugly, with sallow cheeks, and a purple veiny nose. We want them – killers, sex offenders – to be ugly, balding, short, pudgy, double-chinned. We want them to look like the John Doe from *Se7en* – another Spacey character. I guess we want them to look like Kevin Spacey. It makes it that much easier to condemn and punish, the evil within having found its way to the surface.

He abducted the baby from a drug-addicted mother, he said. She didn't deserve this precious gift, he said. But the kidnapped baby cried, as babies will cry, from malnourishment, nappy rash, tiredness, separation. And he said the baby's crying 'annoyed' him, 'you know, like an alarm clock that doesn't have a snooze button.'

We had circumstantial proof but wanted a confession of the baby's murder to remove all doubt. The interview had stalled. Smith was becoming increasingly agitated, but maintained a practiced, meditative calm, standing over Doe from behind, talking softly in his ear, a hiss, as if he were trying to sweettalk him, get him into bed. 'What happened to the baby?' he asked, barely audible, as if for Doe alone.

Silence, except for the white-knuckled clenching of Smith's fingers on the plastic back of the chair.

'What happened to the baby?' Smith whispered again. 'C'mon, you can tell me.'

Again nothing, more clenching, but the volume and tempo of Smith's breathing was on the rise.

It was Smith who cracked first. He screamed into Doe's ear with all the malice of someone who was done playing nice: 'WHAT HAPPENED TO THE BABY?!' accenting each word as if he were talking to a foreigner assumed to be both stupid and deaf. 'WHAT . . . HAPPENED . . . TO . . . THE . . . BABY?!' he screamed again, before picking up a nearby chair and throwing it against the wall with a clatter.

But that wasn't all. Smith's interrogatory *coup de grace* was when he pulled out a photo of the dead child and shoved it in Doe's face. 'THIS BABY!'

Doe turned away from the photo like a child who didn't want to eat a spoonful of mashed vegetables. *Here comes the aeroplane.*

'Take a break, Smith,' I said, drawing the spotlight to play my part. Smith met my eyes, understood that just maybe he had overstepped, at least in view of the cameras which were always keeping score. Or maybe he had got it just right. He tossed the photo on the table and exited, leaving the two of us – me and Doe – in the room which was still humming with Smith's words, the thrown chair and the pulsing wild energy.

I hadn't seen this photo, or any from the crime scene, kept from me the whole time. For good reason, it turned out. Absently, I looked at the photo and saw a blur of grey and yellow. A dead child, a dead infant. Maynard was born pink, with life. When you pressed his skin, it went white and then returned to pink. Life. Not yellow. Not grey. A wave of vomit rose, bitter glands tightening in my throat. I swallowed hard to keep it down, breathing deep, counting down from five like I had been told. Doe looked at the photo, too, passively, indifferent, the baby seemingly a figure he didn't recognise, even when the background had patterns from his home's wallpaper and carpet.

I gave him time for it to sink in. Which didn't take long, as within a minute or so he spoke. 'Do you remember that old Neil Young song, "Keep on rockin' in the free world"?'

I tried hard to compose myself despite the queer question. 'Maybe. I don't know it all that well.'

'There's a verse that I like best.'

And then Doe began to sing. Not at all like Neil Young, but in a high, castrato voice, like that of a choir boy, a voice that nevertheless tremored under the strain of an older man's dirty, withered vocal cords. I won't sing it for you but it was the verse about the woman who hides her baby away to take a hit and how the kid will suffer a pained life, unloved, uncool. When Doe was done, there was a new silence, one that reverberated in a way similar to the silence that followed Smith's tirade. This silence, though, was far more striking and jarring, the tone having slipped from tense to ridiculous. And it would change once more when again he spoke.

'I killed it,' he said. 'The baby. The boy. Just with my hands. The lightest touch.' He said it softly, meekly, with his head hung as if exhausted by the burden of truth.

I was unprepared for the admission, more so than the song, or even the photo. I want to say that I was enraged by what he said, his cold, blunt confession. I want to say that an animal violence was awakened in me, and that I swung my fist at his vulnerable head and beat in his skull, just with my hands, to see his brain, dig my fingers into it, get it under my nails, to know the brain capable of doing what was unimaginable, maybe find the elusive Oedipal complex, dissect it, carve it up with my ready-to-hand pocket knife, see where evil resides, look beyond the ugly surface. In that moment, I thought I was capable, I had it in me. But I didn't. Instead, I froze, in a state of shock like I hadn't known before. I could hardly breathe out, or speak, or move, except to clinically, methodically, write down the precise time and the exact words of his confession in my note pad, concentrating on the scratching of my pen, the hooks and loops, painstakingly crossing *t*'s and dotting *i*'s before glancing over my shoulder to check that the camera in the corner of the room were still blinking red, recording it all, and imagining Smith behind the two-way glass rubbing his hands together cartoonishly, having finally got his man.

John Doe sat silent, hunched over, for several moments as I wrote, until suddenly and sharply raising his head, as if stung. He stared at me, clearly changed, his passive blank eyes now frantic, terrified. 'How can I be judged?'

'What do you mean? At trial?'

'No. How *can* I be judged? By God. Our Maker. How can *I* be judged by the one who made me?'

Like our discussion on Neil Young, questions of God and moral responsibility were not the subjects I was expecting that day and so my response was somewhat perfunctory. 'I can't give you that answer, I'm sorry. Between you and Him.'

'No. No! You don't understand. It is *I* who will judge *Him*, because it is *He* who has made me a child-killer.' His eyes darted back and forth, concentrating deep on my own, to see that his revelation had found its mark. And then he smiled, as if suddenly absolved, as if the matter had been sorted, squared away, the forthcoming trial merely for show, regardless of the confession. He relaxed, reclining as best he could in the cuffs and hard plastic chair, effectively bringing his side of the interview to a close, for him his admission less important than the pact he made with himself against his god.

In that moment I too had undergone what might be described as a significant 'spiritual' change, which would run a line between my past and my future, between my older self and the self of now. In that moment I had become a new kind of selfish, had narrowed the scope of what I could care for and what I couldn't. There was now this and only this. There was only Maynard. [*In her chair, eyes closed, Petal nods her agreement.*]

Smith returned with an officer to lead John Doe away – pulled him up not so gently, holding his arms behind like he were being tortured by the estrapade. Smith gave me a thumbs-up for a job well done. Little did he know that I was unable to stand let alone assist. I finished up writing my report, and by the end of the day I had essentially quit the force for a second and final time.

There were whispers from some who said it was postnatal depression that sent Quinn back to work so quickly, leaving me at home with Maynard; that and the historically short-sighted undertones that she was a cold and unfit mother, not a 'real' woman, if you can believe it. The truth was nothing like that. Every day she mourned leaving her child at home for work, like anyone that had found this undisputable love in their heart. And even if this were only half the truth, how I understood it was that she was letting me take care of the child that I had lost in that final case. She would restore my faith in humanity by allowing me to take care of a small piece of it and keep an eye. And a son needs his father, and a father needs his son.

I pause to take some water. Petal is up and fussing with my leg, checking the bandages and my pulse, not bored but busy. 'You need to take a break, I think. We don't want to get you over-excited.'

'It's distressing when I say it out loud. I can hear it, too.'

'If that's so, then maybe it will remind you why you should call some-body. Before I do.'

I look at my phone on the bedside table. 'Soon. At the right time. I promise.'

Twelve days until his birthday: Inspection of Richie's house

I had a head start with the detectives for this case having al-ready done most of the groundwork and Smith giving me access to Richie's file, but there were my own interviews to conduct, questions to ask. The missing, like the dead, cannot speak. And even before they were missing, at home, sitting on the couch, at the dinner table, existing within the bubble of their family and close friends, they still may have chosen not to speak, or tell much of themselves or who they really are. It is a strange thing that we can never really claim to know anyone else. Even Quinn, my wife for over fifteen years, my best friend, lover, soul mate, mother to my child, BAE, hasn't told me everything about herself and I imagine she never will, just as I have things I haven't told and won't tell. We are our own censor, keeping secrets, keeping to ourselves the things that we know would change how others think of us. And even if we were to tell everything, every detail, we're still limited by our own imagination, our qualities as storytellers, and struggle to convey what is most essential to what we tell.

I cannot claim to know the missing; instead, I attempt to create their stories by collecting their stories from others, those that re-member the missing, and those that remember the past of the miss-ing. Kim emailed me a list of all the people Richie interacted with:

family, friends, work acquaintances – anyone he had contact with. But I was also looking to speak with those characters from his further past. I wanted to find the place of return, and those who knew him best might also know this place, especially those from long ago. My hunch, then, was that Richie had disappeared to a place where those who know him now will have little to do with.

I also needed to trawl through his social media accounts: Facebook, Twitter, Instagram, even his defunct Myspace if he had one. There are also messages, email addresses, and online histories, all of which reveal the trivial to the dirtiest little secret. Anything that has been searched for, shared, downloaded, copied, or saved. Richie didn't have much of an online presence of his own, with very few posts, comments, or likes, and yet it was being kept alive by friends and acquaintances who tagged him in their posts – the will of others maintaining his digital existence. His search histories were deleted daily so I would need permission to hack his accounts. Indeed, there is very little of our digital presence that we can hide. Only if you keep those most important and intimate thoughts offline, stored safe within the grey coral folds of the hippocampus, where taboo and confessions reside, only then might you be able to maintain your privacy, lock away your essence for no others to see.

I wanted photos too, like those in the Allstars box. I had asked Kim to see if she could get hold of more photos from friends under the pretence that they would feature on a collage at his fortieth. Digital photos weren't always useful because of the ease and cheapness of taking them, the result being that too many are taken, resulting in an excess of documentation, which blurs the moment, diluting its consequence. I wanted the old photos, those found on rolls of film, the unique photos, one offs, the opportunistic, the candid, which had a habit of sticking firm in the memory.

And there are also the objects of the missing, their things, their Rosebuds, which can take some digging to find. Some may be in plain sight, whereas some are left all over the place, haphazard and random, like breadcrumbs thrown in a swathe to ducks. But with the right kind of eyes, you can see that the fall of the breadcrumbs leads to a destination, a meaning. The journalists' Rosebud in *Citizen Kane* was spoken by Kane himself, straight from the dying horse's mouth. A significant head start, more of a head start than any of the files on Richie could offer. But I did have a Rosebud of sorts: the Temple of the Dog t-shirt. And there were the other items of Richie's 'costume' – the Allstars and the flanno – which complemented the timeframe in which Richie may have disappeared; a place and time where his getup was contemporary, and hardly considered fancy dress. Though they weren't without their own complications. For both the missing and criminals alike, the 'last seen wearing' details give the public some reference point to help spot them in a crowd, on security cameras. Inevitably, though, time passes and the clothes become a distraction because they are transitory, just as a beard or hair can be grown or cut. The last-seen outfit is a disguise, or, more appropriately, a *guise,* a façade. Language is unhelpful here, for a *disguise* is not a dis-façade and is, instead, a furthering of the guise. His clothes were no guise – they were an accurate representation of the man he longed to be. Or were they disguising the man he was? The '90s was so buried in irony that it was often hard to tell what anyone really felt and what anything meant. The Chucks, the Converse Allstars, exemplified this kind of wild goose chase. Basketball shoes were big in the '90s. Every kid in my neighbourhood wanted a pair of Air Jordan Vs – a bunch of short, weedy, white kids fetishizing over a pair of shoes thinking they too could 'be like Mike.' Not to mention kids in the US were being shot for their shoes, stolen right off their dead feet. In their former life, the Chucks too had been a basketball shoe, one of the first, but by the '80s and '90s they had become less sporting wear and more counter-cultural icon. They never seemed to go out of fashion either, constantly being reappropriated, generation after generation. Today, a fifty-year-old hipster lawyer could be wearing the same Allstars as the thirteen-year-old girl heading to Boost Juice. I got my first pair of Allstars in 1993, age fifteen, from a cross promotion between Jim Kidd's sports stores and Uncle Toby's. I bought them from the Jim Kidd's in Fremantle, between a few games at Quasar and a Fast Eddie's burger for lunch. Black hi-tops with white soles and white laces. As soon as I had them out of the box, I threw them down the road, kicked them along the curb, to scuff them up, take the shine off. I wanted to look like Kurt Cobain who is seen wearing them in many photos. I wanted to look like I had been kicked along the curb, scuffed up. But it's hard to look anti-establishment when you have a pair of scissors in your hand to cut out the barcode from a box of choc-chip muesli bars to get $10 off an already very cheap pair of shoes. With this in mind, how do we compare the meaning of those shoes, my shoes in 1993, to the young girl slurping on 3000 calories worth of cordial at Boost Juice today? What do they mean to the lawyer hipster today, be it their first pair of Chucks or their tenth? This was the problem of the shoes.

The flannelette shirt was another as it can be bought just about anywhere, from the bargain basements to the brand-name boutiques, with the only difference being how much you were prepared to spend. The cheap ones were utilitarian, rough, practical, fit like a sack, whereas the expensive ones were fitted, had special buttons and tabs, to fold the sleeves up, keep them tight. In the '90s, in Seattle, the musicians and punters wore them because it was cold outside, and they took them off and tied them around their waist when they were inside because it was warm. Kurt Cobain is wearing one on the back cover of Nirvana's debut album *Bleach*, having thrown himself into (pre-Dave Grohl) Chad Channing's drum kit. Over time, just like the Allstars, the humble pragmatic flanno became another victim of the hybridisation of mainstream and counter-culture.

This is why Richie's clothes were different. They were a costume, a guise, but not a disguise. The shoes, the flanno, and jeans can still be bought today, separately and mixed and matched with other items, disparate, clashing or otherwise. Still, it gave me a place and time in which he had located himself. Not as a joke or a call back or an exaggeration like other decades-themed parties. If you were a teen in the '80s then you might dress up like Robert Smith of the Cure, tizzed out hair and eyeliner, or Madonna, with a head band or pointed bra, or throw on some leg warmers, skinny tie, have a laugh at how silly everyone looks, saying over and over again that you can't believe we used to dress like this. If it were the '70s you'd be wearing flares, bell bottoms, paisley shirts, throw some flowers in your hair. Or you might go for the late '70's disco craze with platforms shoes, and a John Travolta *Saturday Night Fever*-inspired suit. As Kim had shown, the '90s could be fun too, with plenty of fodder for a piss-take. But Richie's getup was as serious as it comes, with the heroin chic of a junked-up lumberjack.

The interviews would come, but first I wanted to get a feel for Richie's daily routine, his space, his movements, which is why I arranged to visit Kim's home first thing the following day. I needed her and the kids out for a while so that I could be free to trawl through his things, itemise them, create an inventory, weigh up what each item meant to them, from the most mundane to the most treasured. Kim agreed reluctantly, having just met me over a brief coffee – a stranger is a stranger no matter what their title or recommendation.

I was expected at 900 AM, enough time for them to vacate the home. Quinn was dropping Maynard at school, allowing me to get there an hour early, parking a bit down the road, just to see what could be seen. The girls left not long after I arrived. They were on foot, walking to school, heads down, immersed in their phones, the youngest five or so steps behind. Kim waved them off from the door, again dressed in her activewear. She went back inside for 20 minutes or so before emerging from the carport in a black Landrover, presumedly to head to the gym or to meet her PT class. I waited until just before nine, left my car where it was parked and walked up the street and on to the expansive driveway of their early 1900s federation style, heritage-listed character home. From the outside, it looked to have at least four or five bedrooms. There was a white picket fence, rosebushes, and brick pathways running between patches of thick buffalo grass, which might have been considered unruly, given the neighbourhood, but perfectly fine to the casual observer. The brickwork was freshly rendered and tuck-pointed, the front door ornate with stain-glassed roses. I found the key Kim had left under the WELCOME mat and let myself in.

Inside, there was the strong smell of fresh paint coming from the walls – hard white – framed by elaborate ornamental architraves, cornices, and skirting boards. The original Jarrah floorboards of the hallway entrance thudded under my shoes, and weathered Persian runners along the halls softened the spaces between. In the living room, on one wall, above a brown patent-leather modular lounge was a lithograph of Munch's *The Scream*, and on another, above a maybe-replica Eames lounge chair was another lithograph, something cubist, Picasso-esque. The latter picture, if the intention was indeed cubist, might be interpreted as an attempt to capture movement and dimension in the still, flat medium of oil and acrylic; the former, also still and flat, is often interpreted as a being (a homunculus to be specific), frozen by anxiety and the 'the infinite scream passing through nature.' I'd always had an affinity for *The Scream*, ubiquitous as it is in popular culture and famous because of its many thefts, but this version, this framed lithograph, enamoured me even more, as it embodied the problem of my thesis, what with the subtle clash of existentialism and the pomo: Munch provided the existential, the anxiety of the human condition, whereas the imitation and reproduction of the lithograph – right down to the picture-framer's brushed finish giving texture and the faux existence of Munch's hand – screams of the reproducibility and superficiality of a Warholian late capitalism.

From the living room, I moved to the kitchen. It was not original, in its third or fourth iteration, this one being the most modern, sleek and shiny, straight out of the reno reality shows, the 'hero' feature being the new-old copper pipes, green-rashed, conspicuously bringing and draining water and waste, respectively.

There was a dog out the back, a fattish out-of-work kelpie, which barked dutifully, if not half-heartedly, for a minute or so, before conceding to my presence. It made a few turns on the doormat, before tucking its legs and rump underneath itself and promptly fell asleep.

Like many houses at this time of day, theirs was permeated with a particular quiet and stillness that follows the business of a family having left for work or school. There is also a solemnity and esoteric sacredness to both the cleanliness and, maybe more so, the untidiness of the home: beds unmade, cupboards open, breakfast dishes waiting in the kitchen sink, yesterday's dirty clothes in linen baskets, TV remotes left amongst the cushions of the lounge, thrown on the lounge, in disarray. This is why there is such an overwhelming sense of violation when we are burgled. We leave our homes in a very unique state of disorder, one that represents *our* movements, *our* beings, frozen in time, until we enliven it again when we return, to prepare our meals, pick up the remote and turn on the TV, add to the pile of unwashed clothes. The stranger, though, has disturbed the peace, having invaded the sanctity of our suspended lives.

But I am worse than any thief, with my eye for what is most intimate, not interested in the pawnable, the fencable, or really anything that could be easily replaced under house insurance.

Kim said that Richie's birthday party clothes had come from a box in the attic, so I looked there first. It wasn't so much a room, but a reclaimed roof cavity in the American style, with a pull-down step ladder, the kind you find in horror films, classics such as *The Exorcist*, and more recently *Hereditary*. Kim never went up there for that very reason.

The slanted exposed beams looked like some giant beast's ribcage. But this was hard to see, given that the belly was full with many, many boxes and things. One box contained a Christmas tree, the fake plastic leaves poking out from the bulging top. There were two boxes with ornaments. There was also an old black TV, fat and heavy and obsolete, the kind of object that holds no real value, destined to be thrown out but never gotten around to because of idleness or ignorance of how it could be recycled. Another cardboard box was overflowing with electrical cords from old speakers, cables for computers, routers, modems. These were the everyday things that seem to have some practical use, but will never be used, and inevitably just adds to the clutter. Or these things are like a dead, pretty-feathered bird brought to your doorstep by a misguided cat. Too little and too precious to simply chuck in the bin, but not so special as to channel any more time or energy into an empathetic disposal.

Next to the box of cables was another filled with old games consoles, joysticks, controllers. A Commodore 64, an old Sony

PlayStation. Like toys, these do have inherent value but will never be fully utilised other than in a singular nostalgic fix, before scanning eBay to see if they are actually worth anything.

What was of far greater interest was three big boxes of CDs. Hundreds of them, thousands of dollars' worth, from when they sold for $30 each. Most of my collection, other than what I had found the other day, was also in boxes at home, but had been painstakingly digitalised and made portable, the genius of the iPod. Like myself and possibly anyone who lived across the two formats, it is hard to decide on whether it is right to get rid of our CDs. How can they be disposed of, not only in the physical sense (what if the digital copies are accidentally deleted?) but in the nostalgic sense? I am yet to find out. There is also a tangibility to the CD and its cover, only inferior to that of vinyl records, where the grooves of the huge black disk, its topography, provides the visible sense of the band's existence.

Amongst Richie's collection were Temple of the Dog, Soundgarden, Pearl Jam, Nirvana, Alice in Chains, Mudhoney, Hole and a bunch of Sonic Youth albums which, alongside Pearl Jam, were probably the most prolific bands of the era. Sonic Youth: Kim Gordon's agonised, packet-a-day vocals alternating with Thurston's more delicate, soothing tone, the fuzz and distortion of the meandering guitars. Did Richie marry Kim because of her name? Was he looking for someone that resembled physically or nominally the lead singer of one of his favourite bands? It's not uncommon. My Maynard was named after Maynard James Keenan, the lead singer of prog-rock legends Tool. I had to fight for it, and Quinn eventually capitulated, having vetoed the alternatives of Kurt, Chris, Eddie, Layne, and Scott, amongst others. Maybe Richard was named after Richie from *Happy Days*. Richie Cunningham: the good-natured, sensible friend to all, from Ralph-Malph to the Fonz. Not out of the question. And no more ridiculous or self-indulgent, or unfortunate legacy for any child. Or for settling on a Kim, any Kim.

There was also the CD of Pearl Jam's live recordings, *Live on two Legs* (1998), which is when it hit me that I *had* heard the Neil Young verse that John Doe had sung in the interrogation room, just this same verse, covered by Pearl Jam in the breakdown of 'Daughter', slowed down, darker, almost unrecognisable. Unwanted coincidence bells were ringing, as was my own uneasiness at the thought that Doe and Eddie Vedder may have chosen to sing that exact same verse for precisely the same purpose; if not the same ends, then the same means.

There was also the plastic box with his old clothes, the one from which he'd taken his outfit. The box had 'VINTAGE' written in black felt pen on the lid. This seemed a little unfair until I saw that, under a few different-coloured flannos and denim boardshorts, was a safari suit from the 1970s, a few thinning, balling nylon shirts and two pairs of wide-cuffed pants straight from the sixties. Maybe 'RETRO' or 'KITSCH' was more appropriate, but 'retro' was a dirty word these days, and 'kitsch' was too pretentious, and both have undertones of trying too hard, of choosing them because they have returned as fashionable, and not because you had always fancied the style. Vintage, you might say, like 'classic', has a sense of 'always is,' not 'once again.'

Towards the back corner of the cavity, near the window skylight (slightly ajar), there were two milk crates, one for sitting, and the other fixed with a plastic cutting board. On top of the board sat an ashtray, Tally-Ho rollie papers, a Bic lighter, and a handful of joint roaches. There were two old tins: a Quality Street chocolates tin containing the remnants of a marijuana stash and some other bits and pieces for smoking; the other was a Milo tin which was empty except for a few coins. It smelled of money. Maybe he had saved some cash over the years, dribs and drabs, not necessarily missed from a shared bank account with Kim, but could amount to something sizable over time. Maybe this was how he was surviving, on cold hard cash, which, had he indeed decided to flee the scene, had the added benefit of leaving nothing in the way of a money trail.

I itemised what I found in my Moleskin and left the attic to trace his steps through the home, follow the path he would take every day. From his bed when he wakes, to the toilet, to the kitchen, to the kettle. This is not necessarily who he is, his steps, but in Kim's absence my only frame of reference is my own. If he were to wake, put the kettle on before going to the toilet, then he may indeed be a very different person to myself. Or we are exactly the same. I went to the cupboard for cereal. There was Sultana Bran, Froot Loops and muesli. I looked for a bowl and spoon and drew the milk from the fridge, but stopped short from actually putting the breakfast together. The kitchen table looked out on to a large backyard, just smaller maybe than a quarter acre, like the backyard many of us – the middle-aged and older – grew up in. The kind with lots of grass and the Hills Hoist, which always got in the way of me and my brother's game of backyard cricket. The same old rules: over the fence and out; one hand, one bounce. I could see it clearly. A Grey Nicholl's cricket bat for Christmas, single scoop, much thinner and lighter than the pieces of lumber they use today. Did Richie have a Gray Nicholl's or were they an SS or Kookaburra family? Did he put electrical tape on a tennis ball to create some swing? Did he see the same, recall the same, as he looked out from the kitchen table? He has no brother, so a neighbour kid would need to step in and make up the numbers. Is this what he might remember?

From the kitchen table, I could look east. The house was built on a rise and the morning sun could stream in at breakfast. He would watch it rise, maybe; or he might pull the blinds if it were too hot. Maybe, instead of pulling the blinds, he faced the other way so that it didn't get in his eyes, the full sun, bright, strobing through swaying branches of the gumtrees in the yard, as it was doing as I sat there. He could watch Kim and his daughters making their breakfast. Do they rise at the same time? Does Kim ricochet around the kitchen like Quinn does, or does she take her time, prepare herself a shake or smoothie, which is what I imagined. I doubt the daughters eat the Sultana Bran, or the Froot Loops, both of which are well past their 'best before' dates, suggesting that they are at an age where calories are a concern. The muesli is for him, which he eats occasionally but superiorly.

Was there any discussion at breakfast? Do they talk, the kitchen filled with happy chatter? Is it a happy home? Or is the house as it is now, silent, save for the trickling of a small red-clay waterfall outside. I think of the white noise app we bought for Maynard, one of the many weapons against his restlessness, along with a vaporiser, the nightlight, the mobile, and many other newborn essentials, as well as some well-intentioned but unnecessary gadgets and gimmicks. Our families, Richie's and mine, were at different stages, just as our roles were very different. At breakfast, I am in my trackies, old t-shirt, old bathrobe (if it's cold), and Ugg boots. I imagine he is in his suit (maybe he showers before breakfast) with his tie cast over his shoulder like the tail of a scarf to keep it from dangling in his breakfast.

Maybe not so different. Only a few years ago a muslin spitrag would have been cast over my shoulder in a similar fashion as I burped Maynard, protection against the warm milky vomit that often comes, gently jiggling him as I ambled to and fro in the hallway, his sweet, soft breath at my ear, his malleable ribs resting on my collarbone. Ambling and swaying side to side, as mums and dads do with a baby in their arms, and sometimes without, after they grow, as if it were the natural flow and momentum of life that only a baby sets in motion.

Another shoe box (Adidas Gazelles, maroon, like Renton's from *Trainspotting*) was on the dining table, having been brought down (Kim told me), not from the attic, but from high in one of the cupboards, on the top shelf, waiting next to summer doonas packed away for the winter, and winter doonas in the summer. The little treasure chest, this shoebox, was about as close as one can get to a personal archive. When we are born, this task falls onto the shoulders of our parents, the collating and cataloguing of our lives. They do so right up until a certain age, when the child leaves home, or sometimes long after, when, finally, they say: 'The objects that mark your achievements have been hitherto collected for you. However, from now and hereafter it is up to you alone to decide what is special. We can no longer decide for you what to keep and what to discard. We have remembered for you. We have archived your life. And here it is.'

This Adidas shoebox was Richie's humble archive. And this is what I found:

Three baby teeth in a silk pouch.

A souvenir teaspoon from Kalgoorlie, a golden embossed Paddy Hannan on the handle.

A commemorative coin for the 1988 bicentenary, from his primary school days.

A key to a padlock, Lockwood.

A watch; Casio. Missing the band, stopped; a feathering crack in its face.

A ticket stub from a Soundgarden concert. Another from Pearl Jam, and Stone Temple Pilots. One from Sonic Youth.

A photo of Richie about to blow out candles on his fifth birthday, grinning baby-toothed to the camera. A bunch of kids surrounding him, eyes only for a cake that is iced in Spiderman red and blue.

The teeth could have been his daughters'. We have kept all of Maynard's teeth including those that smashed on the climbing frame. Most parents probably do. The teeth might even be Richie's. My mother presented mine to me on my twenty-first and I still have them which is kind of strange when I think about it. What we do with Maynard's is anybody's guess.

Like the electrical cables kept upstairs, the key and watch were either useless or unneeded and yet full of potential: one day the padlock that matches the key will be found and will perform its function once again; and the watch – an intricate piece of machinery, which should be respected as such – could be repaired; but it would be costly, and besides it is not old enough to be considered antique and not uniquely fashionable enough for a rebirth. It may be his first watch, a birthday present. It would then be the embodiment of a formative moment, a new sense of responsibility for something that is precious and delicate. Thus, it stays, useless as it is, and imbued as it is with both hope and sentimentality.

The coin had little of the watch's sentimental value, and yet, like the game consoles, could be worth something one day, maybe, to the collector we imagine is patiently waiting for us to post our treasures online. The coin was the exact same as the one I received in Year 4, 1988, just as every child from that year had received one. If Richie was like me, he was optimistic, believing that the coin's value would increase over time. Problem is the market would be flooded (and the bicentenary hasn't aged all that well).

The teaspoon was of some interest. Had Richie been to Kalgoorlie? A school trip, maybe?

Last but not least were the concert ticket stubs, which only added to my conviction that Richie was gone not only to a place but a time.

But there was something else giving weight to my hunch. As I went through his things, very steadily the light in the dining room and kitchen began to dim, not from a blown globe in the rail of lights above, but more like a shadow had been thrown across the world, as if by a sudden eclipse or cloud that had come from nowhere, crossing in front of the sun on what was expected to be a clear, cloudless sky. But it wasn't an eclipse or a cloud and not properly a shadow either, more a dislocation or an estrangement such that the kitchen and dining area, the space I was in, became unfamiliar, the shadow fog creeping over everything, not altering it physically – everything retained its shape and size – but in my mind they were suddenly unrecognisable. You might argue that in a stranger's house everything is unfamiliar; I would counter this by suggesting that we do know and retain the general layout and look of our surroundings, even when they are new to us. And it felt more like the space, the objects, both his and mine, were being drained of recognition right before my eyes. It swelled, engulfed me, a transparent mental fog, and a sudden oncoming of dread as my chest seemed to hollow out, and my heart, fist-sized with rounded knuckles, started to thump hard, fast, like the onset of a sudden caffeine hit, Red Bull, Dexies, ecstasy, the drop of a techno jungle beat, OD fear. I froze in my place, braced myself, as I felt the world list, a slight giddiness, like a cruise ship rolling on a swell. And then came a wave of paranoia, the feeling that I was being stared at by an unseen crowd huddled at the periphery of my vision, silent and laughing, all at once. I know, by some intuition the reason for them staring: I have shouted or screamed something, broken a public taboo, disrupting the crowd that was minding its own business. And even though I knew in myself that I hadn't screamed, that I hadn't called out, I sensed that I would do so at any moment, unbidden, as if it were inevitable, that I must act to give rise to the reaction that has already come. The only explanation – a bold one – was that I had slipped out of the ordinary passing of time. But only for a moment, as soon the sense of the crowd had vanished and what remained was the overlay of a moment from my past, like déjà vu, which appeared as a half image, a photo negative, the ghost static from an old TV. I knew the moment from my past, the feel of it, but I couldn't see it clearly enough to place it within a context, and I concentrated, trying to grasp it, yet it remained just out of reach, lurking at the corner of my eye and if only I could turn my head quick enough would I catch it, see it for what it is. The moment then is this combination of sublime dread and metaphysical intrigue as to its cause.

It couldn't have been a few minutes if not seconds, as my consciousness resurfaced into recognition, the fog and shadow dispersing. Except that there was the sense of another shadow lurking. It was not a crowd and there was no laughing; instead, it was a singular soft voice, one that quietened all others, gently bringing the world back to itself: 'That's my great, great, great, grandfather.'

'Huh?' I felt drunk and must have looked it as I tried to focus on the figure speaking to me. It was their eldest daughter. 'Sorry, I'm not sure I understand,' I said, feigning composure.

'You were staring at the urn.'

'I was?' and looked to where she was pointing. On top of a Scandinavian sideboard was a dark wooden funeral urn, only slightly larger than the Ashes trophy of the Australia versus England Test cricket series. 'I guess I was. Sophie, isn't it?'

'Emily. Sophie's my younger sister. It's my great, great, great, grandfather. On my dad's side.'

I scrutinised the urn more closely as if the new information would help me better understand its contents. 'Was he a Digger, an ANZAC?'

'No.'

'Oh, I thought he might be someone quite special, a hero maybe?'

'No. He was pretty boring, if you ask me. Dad just didn't want to get rid of the urn. There aren't even any ashes in it. Or there are only some leftovers in there. They were spread in the Baltic Sea or something.'

'Still, there is a trace of someone that holds the same bloodline as you in there,' I said, with unintentional creepiness. If a stranger being caught staring at an urn in your dining area wasn't bad enough, then talking about a young girl's connections to the dead should have made her run out of the house screaming.

But she didn't.

'There are others as well. He collects them. They're in the shed. That's his favourite though. Now that he's gone, I guess they will all be ours or Mum will get rid of them. She's never liked them. Too morbid, she says.'

'You think he's gone? What makes you say that?'

'I have heard Mum talking on her phone. She thinks she is being quiet. She's not.' A smile flashed across her face, and then a giggle, which is when it dawned on me that she was really very stoned. Maybe it wasn't just Richie using the attic.

'I won't say he is gone. Let's just say that he is . . .'

'Gone?!' she said furiously, and the wasted grin was replaced by the scowl from the school-day photo, an eruption of resentment at being treated like a child. An emotion that can be turned outwards, thrown like a dagger, instead of being held on to, like misery and sadness, and the internalised raking of the walls of her stomach.

'Shouldn't you be at school?' I asked, attempting to be inquisitive, but knew immediately that it sounded like an accusation.

She quaked, confronted, but regained (or feigned) her own composure. 'I skipped. There's an app my parents use when we are absent to let the school know. I know the password.'

'I see.'

We regarded each other, a stalemate, only temporary, as her face steadily fell into a frown, and her small hands balled into fists, angry at herself for having said too much. 'Get out of my house!'

she yelled, startling us both by the volume of her command, and how it echoed rudely off the floorboards and walls. It was a warning, that this was not okay, that we were not getting 'cosy', and she hoped that others, neighbours, passers-by, her father, would come save her, throw this intruder out on the street. I was the enemy, one of the many adults who had been lying to her. There to help but not yet one of the inner circles of friends and family that could be trusted. In that moment she reminded me of my big sister, three years older than me. My sister at about the same age as Emily. Precocious, strong-willed, and heartbreakingly vulnerable.

'I am going to go,' I said gently, 'but I must tell you that I will be coming back, just so you know. I will talk to your mum. Not that you were skipping school, and not about the pot you've been smoking, but ask her to talk to you and explain what I am doing here. I need all the help I can get.' I smiled, an olive branch, hoping that some alliance could be formed.

'Okay,' she said, defeat in her voice, and maybe even a little embarrassment. And with that she turned for her room and closed the door, softly.

I gathered my things, and left the house feeling as if I had triumphed, having won over the confidence of a teenage girl, which seemed only slightly easier than that of a serial killer.

Petal is listening, and I had hoped that I would at least get a smile, a titter, or a teehee with the serial killer remark. Instead, she is writing a list in her little spiral-bound notepad. She has underlined one word in particular. It must be serious. She tried to hide it from me, but I saw.

'What are you writing?' I ask, facetiously.

'Oh, nothing.'

'A shopping list?'

'No.'

'A to-do list, then?'

'No, just some thoughts.'

'Are you diagnosing me?'

'No.'

'But I can see that you have written some big words. One of them starts with an "s". Is it . . . schizophrenia?'

'I can't say.'

'Let me put your mind at ease. Quinn, my expert clinical psychologist wife with lots of letters after her name would know if I had psychosis, bi-polar disorder, or schizophrenia – underlined.'

'So, you've told your wife about this "instance"?'

'No, not everything.'

'Hmm. That's all well and good for you to decide what you tell your wife, but I wouldn't be doing my job properly if I let this piece of information slip through. It clearly sounds like there is something going on. I don't know what, but I will need to let someone know about it.'

'You might be right, and maybe I can shed some more light on it for you, but it's best that we don't be too hasty in drawing our conclusions.'

'Please do explain it for me. I'm listening. But this is ink I'm writing in and I only write my notes once.'

What happened at Richie and Kim's house was not the first time. And now might be the right time to disclose the real reason for me taking this case with such urgency. I was not a psychic, or psychic detective, as Kim had implied. And I'm certainly not like the Patricia Arquette character in *Medium* or Jennifer Love Hewitt in *The Ghost Whisperer*. I cannot see into the future and I cannot speak to the dead. But I was convinced that I did have some sort of 'gift' which seemed, at particular instances, to connect me with a realm beyond the experiential world. [*Petal is underlining schizophrenia again. I can't help but admire her stoic adherence to the rationality of the DSM-5.*]

The earliest I remember was when I was 15. I kept it to myself thinking it was just a one-off. But they kept happening, more frequently, although still months apart. Mostly they were mild, which is how I would describe the 'episode' at Richie's. This might seem a bit out of left field, but it is a little like Roquentin's experience in *Nausea*, by Jean-Paul Sartre – my chosen philosopher and existential hero, if you will (I have a caricature of him in my study, watching me always, lazy-eyed). Roquentin's familiar world was no longer so: forks and doorknobs have become estranged, and so have people, and bodies, bringing with it a nauseous feeling. This description comes close to what I experience; however, unlike Roquentin, my experiences are temporary, not a permanent reconfiguration of the existence of things.

Some episodes are more severe. They begin the same, but instead of having some 'sense' of familiarity, I lose all recognition of where I am, or who I am. The earliest I remember was when I was 17, heading home from school, walking from where the bus dropped us off. I remember the shadow, the draining of all familiarity, until I had no idea where I was or where I was going. It was as if I had no history in that place, a parallel world in which I had never previously existed. Or, if I existed, then both my short and long-term memory had been emptied, wiped clean. I sat on the curb, no more than five houses from the home I had lived at my whole young life, waiting for my world to come back to me. It took maybe five to ten minutes, and I found my way home. After these incidents, I'd go about my day feeling slightly ill, clouded by a low-grade migraine, and walk awkwardly, as if my path were a series of stepping stones, with the stride between them being too long and too short at the same time.

Only when I moved in to detective work, did it feel like it could be of some use. Smith said it was my cop's gut instinct that helped me, but there was something else, some other kind of instinct that was working with the theory, something that refined the search, like playing 'hot and cold'. And for my detective work, it felt more like having seen what someone else had already seen. More than this: it felt as if it were not merely a replication of the past but a call from the past, as if it were trying to reach me. As if nostalgia were calling me back, to do it right, to rewrite, and correct the past. Something, a moment from the past, reminding me of itself. Not just mine, but others' too; it was the missing's past that I was seeing, which is why it didn't always make sense.

This is why I haven't told many people before – it sounds crazy. [*Petal is nodding in agreement*]. But that is part of my story, not Richie's, so let us return to the world of his past.

Eleven days until his birthday: Meeting with Smith

After my visit to their home and the déjà vu episode, I felt that it was about time I talked to Smith, get his take on the case and find out what else he knew about Kim. He had interviewed her several times before, and I was ready to compare notes.

Smith had recommended me for only four cases in the six years since I left the force, all classified as 'long-term missing persons' with little to no media interest. They were cold cases, having exceeded the initial three months of searching. This was why Smith's recommendation of Richie's case was unusual: it had only been six weeks and he was already looking for alternatives.

As a rule, we met at a coffee shop just down the road from the station, central Northbridge, away from those unfriendlies within the force who might send a whisper to Internal Affairs that I was getting myself involved in something I had no business with. I left the force on good terms, but I know that I had lost some leeway, deemed weak, not up for proper hardcore policing; in their eyes I was now more civilian than cop.

We were at the little round tables outside of the cafe, near the street, the traffic keeping strangers from getting hold of our private conversation. Smith is in his late fifties, gave up smokes ten years ago, alcohol three years ago, has cut his red meat down by half and the general itch that pervaded his demeanour told me the absence of all three wasn't quite working for him.

'You look like shit,' I said, an ice-breaker of sorts, as we waited for our coffees to arrive. We didn't small-talk much. We probably should have tried, get out of our heads a little, but there was also a keep-a-distance mentality that most cops had, an emotional safe-guard, just in case something goes wrong; and lots can go wrong. In the last ten years, Smith hadn't even been to my home or me to his. He hadn't met Maynard, and probably couldn't spot Quinn in a line-up for that matter. He never seemed interested, which didn't really bother me.

'I look like shit?' Smith said, a wry smile on his face, massaging the two-day stubble on his jaw, the deep wrinkles on his forehead sitting high in exaggerated surprise. 'You must be looking into a mirror, my boy. Not sleeping again?'

'Every now and then.'

'Waste of time anyway, if you ask me. Always someone doing something wrong out there.' With that, Smith straightened in his chair, squared his shoulders, and fixed his eyes on me. Polite conversation was over. 'So?'

'So, I feel like I'm early to this, a little premature.'

'You are, but that's because something isn't sitting right. Austin and Richie are both dirty but whichever way we cut it, there is nothing to suggest much of anything.'

'You don't think it was about money?'

'I didn't say that exactly.'

'Are you thinking Kim had something to do with it?'

Smith wasn't surprised by the question. 'You've met her, you've been to their house. You tell me.'

'She seems harmless. No obvious antipathy towards him, genuine grief.'

'I felt the same when I first met her. But there was something off. Just a show for us cops. That was my guess.'

'Murder, then?'

Smith thought on the possibility, but not for the first time. 'Could well be. His life insurance was all paid up. Took care of accident and suicide too. Big, big dollars. But there's no money from a missing person. You need a body for that payday.'

'A second family? Maybe he abandoned their debts, the life, the pretence of the well-to-dos, for a simpler working-class family-life?'

'That sounds a lot like my life and I would happily trade places if he's looking to downgrade.'

Our coffees came. Smith poured three sachets of NutraSweet into his straight black coffee, and, disregarding the nearby spoon, stirred it with his finger, which would've hurt a lot more than he let on.

'Was he sick? Cancer, something inoperable?' I said, watching him wipe the wet finger on a paper napkin.

'I'd considered that. If she knew, she wasn't letting on. Kept the medical records real tight to her chest. But it makes a whole lotta sense if he was.' Smith paused a while, his eyes searching, the look of someone rolling bubble gum with their tongue, rolling something around in his brain. 'Makes a lotta sense.'

Cars and buses slid past with a whoosh, giving rise to a pause in the conversation, and a chance for me to skew the subject. 'What do you know about the '90s?'

'What, the 1990s? The decade the '90s? What's to know. I got married, had three kids, got divorced, got married, inherited two other kids and then it was 2000. Oh, and the Eagles won two grand finals.'

'Wow, you really are an old man.'

'Careful.'

'What I mean is, how did the '90s *feel?*'

Smith brought his left hand to his mouth, index finger to thumb, an invisible cigarette held between them, before putting his hand down again. 'I can't tell you what it felt like then. But I can tell you now that it seemed as if it were . . . complicated but less complicated too.' He tapped on the table, stubbing out the ghost cigarette. 'I look at it now, after the internet, and wonder how the hell we got anything done. There was so much effort for the smallest piece of information. A street address, shopping, tying a fucking fly to go fishing. Nothing at your fingertips and all I can think was that I must have been pretty stupid. But it was also simple too *because* there was no internet. Meth hadn't taken off, Islamic terrorism wasn't really on the radar, no one worrying about being PC all the time. There was some talk about global warming, the Greenhouse effect and CFCs but it all still seemed within our grasp. You know what I remember about the '90s? I remember being young. And I remember the freedom to be who I was, without question. Absolutely free.'

'A lot has changed since then.'

'Sure enough and it'll keep changing until we no longer recognise a thing about it.'

'I am hopefully meeting Kim again in the next few days and maybe I can get a better idea about her. I also want to find out a bit more about Austin.'

'That's good. See if he's sticking to the same story about the fraud charges.'

'And what about him and Kim?'

'Don't know. I looked into it but nothing to confirm or deny. Which reminds me, you should ask her about Tommy Clayton. See what he knows. Maybe you'll even get a bit of the truth out of her. Six weeks might have also given her time to rethink some of her statements.'

'Tommy Clayton, eh? Another affair?'

'Instead of. His name came up a lot. Might be Kim and Austin, but Tommy is most likely. Either way, someone is sleeping with someone they shouldn't be sleeping with.'

'Do you think Richie knew anything about this?'

'Hard to say. My impression is that the doughy, naïve bastard was just skimming like a stone across the surface of life without any clue whatsoever.'

'That might be true, but I think this affair thing might be going both ways. I reckon he's gone back to find an old girlfriend from high school. Someone who gets him.'

'What makes you think that?'

'A photo.'

'One photo?'

'And a younger man's hunch, amongst others.'

'Well, if that's the case, then Richie might be disappointed. Look how ugly you're getting as time gets hold of ya. Me, I have plateaued handsomely. No looking back for me.'

Tommy hadn't come up before, not from Smith or Kim, and was a surprise. I didn't like being drip-fed the bits of information

I should have up front. I didn't blame Smith. Besides, I was always banging on about how I liked to find things out for myself. He was maybe giving me a bit of stick back, keep me on my toes. Either way it was a good reason to ask Kim to meet again, and as soon as possible. As of that afternoon, there were eleven days until his birthday. And although this was very much an invented, arbitrary countdown, there was pressure to find him, and, dare I say, suspense, possibly because it was unusual: ordinarily we count the number of days that the missing have been missing, not the days that we have left to find them. Unless there is a ransom, and a countdown for payment to be made. But no such information had landed on my desk or Smith's.

Ten days until his birthday

Kim told me she was busy all weekend and that I should come on Monday night when the girls were at netball practice. What she was busy with, she didn't say. Between a few playdates for Maynard, Auskick Sunday morning, and a lunch with Quinn's folks, I spent the weekend organising meetings with Austin and Tommy – Tuesday and Wednesday, respectively.

When I cold-called Austin, he seemed at ease, expectant, and cool. 'I am very glad to hear from you. Like everyone, I'm really concerned about Richie's welfare and would certainly like to help in any way I can. I have had to take on Richie's clients in his absence so I am quite swamped. But I always take a lunch break so come by around 1145, Tuesday. I'll have something prepared. We can eat and talk.' His tone was affable, familiar, easy to like, but he'd clearly highjacked the conversation, the standard technique of a liar. We hung up and I waited a minute before calling him again. Straight to voicemail. Best guess he was on the phone to Kim, scrambling to get their stories straight.

I did a bit more snooping on his social media. Unlike Richie, Austin wasn't shy of the camera, with plenty of photos of him on his social pages. Nor should he have been, handsome as he was, well-groomed and dressed, healthy looking, tanned, salon haircut, teeth that were white and straight. He was, by all appearances, a tremendous success. And he lived only a suburb over from Richie, albeit a step up in affluence. Of course, they worked together too, but they weren't partners; it was Austin's accounting firm. His social media history also showed me that their families were close. Photos of sailing together, at dinners, corporate events, corporate boxes at the football. As close as any middle-aged mates that met after high school can be. Much of it, the pictures, was from a few years back and the feed was more about the kids, a girl and two twin boys. Kim's eldest daughter and Austin's were about the same age and could know each other well enough, even if they were at different schools. Austin's boys looked about one year younger.

Something had happened though. And when I dug a little deeper into his private data, I found that divorce papers had been requested by Jamie, Austin's wife. It hadn't been followed through with, left unsigned by Jamie. They'd made amends, figured out a scenario in which they could stay together, get over this hurdle, reconcile. This might also explain going dark on his socials. But also pointed a finger at a probable cause for a rocky marriage. Was Kim the other woman? Hopefully my meeting with Austin would shed some light on this possible love pentagon, and the one corner missing.

'Are you enjoying not telling me what happens, asking yourself questions, like you don't know the answers.'

'But that's the thing, I don't know the answers. Richie isn't found.'

Petal's arms are crossed. She takes a deep breath and lets out an exasperated sigh.

'This is helping me, giving me clarity. And I'm hoping that you will see something I don't. You're smart, "Seafoam".'

'Oh, please. I'm your nurse, not a detective. But go on, ask yourself as many questions as you like, but stop acting like you don't know the future.'

'I can't guarantee that.'

[Repeat of exasperated sigh with a hint of eye roll.]

Eight days until his birthday: Second meeting with Kim

The weekend passed, Monday night came, and after preparing a kid-friendly, non-chilli-chilli con carne for dinner, was on my way to meet Kim. Again, I arrived early, parked across the road a few houses down. At about half an hour to go, a grey Mercedes SUV pulled into their drive and the two girls came out of the house, jumped in the car and left. Kim was in her athletic wear again, and waved to them from the door, watched the car as it drove away, and then scanned the street, arms folded. She knew I was coming, but not yet. Was she looking for me? Or was she looking for Richie? Was she expecting him to just be casually walking up the street, returning from his walk six weeks ago, having been waylaid by a neighbour for a chat, or that he'd stopped to help a stranger change a flat tyre? Or was she trying to look like she was looking for Richie. Whatever it was, it lasted only a moment, as she rocked on her heels, and returned inside, a show of giving up.

I waited until it was time before approaching her door. From in-side, I could hear Tupac's 'California Love' ending, just as 'Regulate' by Warren G and Nate Dog started up. I didn't expect she would hear my knock but the music quietened and she opened the door. Maybe their kelpie standing next to her sniffed me out, or a hidden camera that slipped my inspection.

Between seeing the girls off and my arrival, she had changed her outfit, and with it looked very different to the woman I'd met at the café. Gone were the leggings and crop-top, replaced with a long yellow floral dress. Her hair was also freed from her cap, and was now full and wavy. Sara Conner from *T2* had returned to the Sara Conner of the '80's original.

'Hello,' she said and waved me in with a smile. 'Would you like a drink? I have red wine, white wine, gin, beer – shit beer and good beer. Water?' She spoke over her shoulder as we made our way down the hall, past the living room, the fake Munch and Picasso, the replica Eames, to the dining room and kitchen, the dog padding slowly behind. Kim was at ease, bubbly even. She could relax, some of the weight having been lifted from her shoulders, knowing that their secrets – hers and Richie's – had been partially laid bare.

'I'm on the clock – yours actually – so water will do,' I replied not-so-seriously.

'Of course,' she said, winking conspiratorially, and motioned that I sit at the dining table. Kim grabbed a tumbler from the dishwasher and filled it up through the filter in the fridge, placed it on a coaster in front of me. She returned to the kitchen bench, and stood behind it, like a dais, empowered.

Again, I was playing the role of Richie, sitting in his chair, and now talking with his wife. And from where she stood, she saw the shape of me as she would have seen the shape of him. We are not that much different in that respect. But I was not a substitute for him. For he still gilded everything, even in his absence. And I could feel traces, still of the déjà vu from the last time I found myself in the kitchen, the dimming, the voices, and dread. All I could do was talk over them, silence them, so that I could be present in the here and now. 'I want to get to know more about Richie, but let's start off easy. Tell me how your story together began.'

'Okay. Well, we met at a work function. A Christmas party, actually. 2004? I had come with a girlfriend. She worked there, I didn't. She was trying to set us up. He was drunk.' Kim smiled distantly, her eyes fixed on a spot on the wall, as if old home videos were being projected onto it. 'We talked and drank. We were so drunk.' Here she laughed, luminescent, white, aligned teeth on show. 'Anyway, he gave me his mobile number and I called the next day and we met up for coffee. He was very quiet, shy. Hungover too, probably. But, also, confident and funny.'

'And what about now?'

'Now, he is a good man,' she said, becoming serious, again with distance. 'Though he has changed a lot. Who hasn't, really? I'm not the same as I was then. But he has changed, more than our friends, more than me, that's for sure. It sounds horrible I know, but he has become very . . . dull. I don't think he was depressed. It was just like he was on autopilot, going to work, watching TV, off to bed early because he said he was tired. He was tired all the time. I'm tired too, you know. What makes him any different?'

She wanted me to untangle the emotions for her: bitterness, confusion, love. A Venn diagram with these three circles overlapping, and Richie at the centre.

'The girls had adored him. He used to read to them, doing all of the voices. He used to braid their hair. But they are pulling away a bit, maybe because they don't have as much in common with him now. They are teenagers or close enough to it, becoming young women. But he was elsewhere, or he didn't want to know. You should have seen when he found out about them getting their periods. Sorry, you didn't need to know that.'

'Perfectly natural.'

'I was worried also because I don't think he was providing a good male role model for them. He didn't cook or clean, but he didn't do anything really. He was a good dad, though. It's just that . . .' She stared at her glass, watching the run of the wine's legs. 'No, that's bullshit if I'm honest. There's no point in flattering him. You want the truth, he was an ordinary father, bordering on shitty. Any dad can be good if they don't beat their kids, or yell at them, or ignore them. If that's the case then, yes, he was a good dad. There are only good dads and bad dads. You know what a good mum is, though? A good mum is just a mum. Just mums. We are expected to be good. You are either a mum or a bad mum.'

She paused, recollected herself, took a deep meditative breath, and closed her eyes. 'He used to have real passion about him, always talking about social injustice, inequality, human rights. Always thinking about others' misfortunes and about how he wanted to make a difference.' She opened her eyes and fixed on mine. 'That's when he was excited about life. This is when he really spoke his truth, when you actually saw some fire in his eyes, a sense of righteousness. It was very attractive, something sexy about it, the whole Che Guevara thing he had going on. But he never did anything about it. He just kept moaning about "our impotence to change things."' Either the wine or resentment had made her flush. 'But that fire has gone, as has the talk of equality, yada yada yada. It gets tired anyway, the whole idealism thing.'

Kim was at ease in her anger, the way she swirled the wine glass in her hand, cocked her hip. I saw an opportunity: 'I have to ask, and please don't take offense, but do you know if he was seeing anyone else?'

The swirling held its momentum, the hip remained cocked, her eyes frowning, staring somewhere over my shoulder. Unfazed. 'Definitely not. No, I just can't imagine it. We still made love every other month, so I guess he still finds me attractive. That's normal isn't it, when you've been married for as long as we have? Tell you the truth, who would have an affair with him? She would have to be pretty desperate.'

My question had hurt, maybe from giving credence to the real possibility of him leaving her for someone else. It could have been a good time to push, ask about Austin or Tommy, but she was working herself up: 'Sex is for the young anyway. Did you know that? Without love and the history and memories of the relationship helping you see past the wrinkly, ugly body, then surely sex should be left to those who are still physically attractive. I work out, I want to look good, too, but there is a point where you no longer exercise to look hot, to keep your husband interested, but to keep your heart healthy and to stop your bones from becoming brittle. I have a few older clients in my PT classes. Sixty- and seventy-year-old women. Do you know what they tell me? They tell me that they aren't exercising to turn their husbands on – they're exercising to make sure they outlive them.

'Don't get me wrong, I miss being desired, by him, by other men. I see them, grown men, looking at my daughters. I want to be desired like my girls are desired. At the same time, I want every one of these fucking perverts to keep their eyes to themselves or I might just cut their tiny little dicks off!'

She was looking elsewhere, caught up, still swirling her wine, which was now in danger of escaping its orbit.

'I looked through the shoe box, the Adidas shoe box,' I said, unsubtly attempting to change the mood.

'Oh, you did? Was there anything else that you found interesting?' she said offhandedly, weirdly uninterested.

'You didn't look?'

'No, I mean not really. I did but it looked like there was nothing important.'

'Some things might not offer much insight. I thought the ticket stubs were interesting and do connect with the Temple of the Dog shirt. He liked grunge, alternative music, I take it: Soundgarden, Alice in Chains, Pearl Jam, and Nirvana – "Come as you were"?'

'That was for his sake, but I wouldn't say I was a fan. So dark. So angry.'

On cue, the preamble of NWA's 1988 'Fuck Tha Police' ghetto-blasted its way over the speakers, before dropping into its infamous, cop-deriding verses.

'Excuse me,' Kim said, a touch embarrassed, 'I only get to listen to this playlist when the girls are out. They are listening to Taylor Swift or Billie Eilish or something, others I can't remember.'

'I don't mind in the slightest. A child of the '90s or thereabouts should have a healthy appreciation for the pioneers of "gangsta" rap', and made a show of the scare quotes in an attempt to acknowledge my unhipness. 'It's how I first learnt about the problems African-Americans were facing in the US. [*Petal raises an eyebrow*]. Or I just liked it for the *Parental Advisory Explicit Lyrics* sticker on the cover.'

'Oh God, yes. Scared the hell out of my parents. I think the stuff Richie liked was bad, but a white girl listening to black guys rapping about guns and hoes was next level.'

She was attractive when she laughed. It would be something that men would try their best to make happen.

'And what about the memento spoon from Kalgoorlie. Had he lived there?'

'No, not Richie. His father had. They had a farm near Manjimup, which is where Richie grew up. The farm was struggling. They were throwing everything at it – cows, sheep, grapes, apples – hoping something would stick. Charlie was offered a job with the hope of making some quick money to get the farm back on its feet. It didn't work out as he hurt his back within a few weeks and came home to let it heal but it never really did. He couldn't work the farm either but by then he was starting to lose his memory, anyway. There were other signs he was getting dementia. When Charlie went into a home, Richie inherited the debt from years of failed seasons of crops. He tried to piece it back by paying a caretaker to tend it for a while, investing in equipment, and make something of the land, all at arm's length.'

I had some of the photos with me. One was the photo of Richie and his big group of friends. I pointed to the tall blonde boy standing next to him. 'Can you tell me who this is?'

She scanned the photo, recognised him. 'That's Steven. He was Richie's best man at our wedding. I never knew him all that well. He was from Richie's Manjimup days. One of his school mates. Before me.'

'Did they have a falling out?'

'I'm not sure, or at least Richie didn't say.' She looked again at the photo, looked at the other faces. She fixed on the girl that had appeared in the other photo, the one of him dancing. 'Do many women go missing? Do they get frightened by turning 40 and abandon their families too?'

This was the first hint that we may have shared an explanation for his disappearance. 'Not many. Actually, I've just had the one female client. Donna, from a few years ago. She was 45 years old, mother of three, empty nester, last seen trying to tizz her hair out, and knitting some multicoloured Fluro leg warmers. And then "poof," suddenly she was gone.'

'You're not being serious, are you?'

'There's some truth there. I got a call from her distraught husband. I visited her home. The house was impeccably clean, well-furnished, like it was ready for an *Inside Out* magazine shoot. Except for the youngest daughter's room. This last daughter had recently turned 18, gotten a placement at UNSW, packed her things and moved out. The husband said it was the shock of the daughter leaving. That there was real tension between him and Donna and their daughter, arguing about how she will support herself and who will she live with and why the Eastern states, what had they done. Was she angry at them? The daughter left for Sydney, and the next day, Donna was gone without a trace. We are still looking for her.'

'That's interesting. I can tell you why there aren't many women that go missing. It's because we are reminded every day that we are aging. [*Petal is furiously nodding her head. I told you so. Women know it.*] Every day. On TV, movies, magazines. Every day, before leaving the house, we spend time looking at ourselves in the mirror, at our faces. We might try to cover it up, makeup, hair dye. We get plastic surgery, cosmetic surgery. But it doesn't come as a surprise to us that we're getting older. Richie would take about five minutes to get ready and probably hadn't looked at himself properly for years. Most days he would shave in his office because he had run out of time here, sleeping in usually. And then, all of a sudden, he is nearly 40 and freaks out. What bullshit. Women get on with it, knowing that they are becoming less attractive, less desirable. A woman's life is an evolution. Men don't even have menopause to worry about. They have a pill to keep them hard like a virile man should be, but nothing can stop menopause, running out of eggs like we have a use-by date.' [*More nodding from Petal.*]

Kim was looking at me, at my face, but was focussed somewhere past my eyes, through me, to the back of my skull. She took a slug from her glass and began speaking of Richie again as if stumbling out of a trance. 'He grew up on the farm but somehow managed to get a part-scholarship at Scotch and was staying at one of the boarding houses near Nedlands which is where I grew up. I went to Perth Ladies College and we had mixers with the Scotch boys which is how we first met.

'So, the work function you told me about earlier was in fact the second time you met?'

She didn't miss a beat. 'I guess it was. Then he disappeared back to Manjimup. And then there he was, at the work do, where we met properly. It wasn't an obvious match. My family did pretty well for themselves, and he had trouble with it; too proud, the farming boy. Especially since the farm was barely surviving. He had the scholarship so he never really fit in with the full-paying boys. We got engaged and as soon as he was chained to my family, he seemed to ease into the lifestyle, accept that we had cash, could do more things with money, fewer limitations. He changed how he spoke, dressed differently. I didn't think much of it at the time. I just thought that was what you did when you matured. We all grew older and change, we all got wiser, more conservative too. But I look back at it now and realise he was adapting to a completely new type of life. He kept his sense of humour and bit of the country boy's ignorance which I loved. There is a bubble we live in around here. He didn't quite understand it at first, but he came around. Listen to me, I am sounding like such a snob.'

'You can't help what you are born into.' A subtle dig, not intended to offend, which, fortunately, she had the good sense of humour to play along with.

'Watch it, or you'll only be getting straight tap water from now on,' she said and laughed attractively. 'You think Richie wasn't a snob too? You should see his passport, where we've travelled. He could make a flight attendant jealous. Which does remind me of something: a few years ago, we went to Switzerland. I remember him saying that he wished he could live there. In the mountains. Because, he said, his mind just emptied and he thought about nothing, remembered nothing, just existed. I'm sure there were photos.

He always loved winter best, the cold, snow, blizzards. He said it was because that was the true weather. Weather, he said, was something we feared, shied away from, but it also made us feel alive. That's what he said.

'He had travelled to the outback – Karajini, Uluru – where it is full of heat and red dust. That was weather too, I said to him. But he said that blue sky was not enough and made the world feel stagnant. That was the word: "stagnant." He said it felt like the world was going on elsewhere and he had to get back to it. I don't know how that was any different to Switzerland. He also said it was too hot to think in the outback. "A man can only lose his mind in the heat," he said, over and over. I was losing my mind from him, not the heat.'

This was an intriguing detail: it had been a long Perth summer and, just when you thought it was over, March had offered up more of the same. Not far-fetched to think that he had spent the whole season planning his escape.

'You think he might have gone to Switzerland, then?' I asked.

'No, no. He wasn't that adventurous, all words and no action. And as I said before, his passport is still here locked in our safe. I've almost worn the numbers off its keypad from checking it so many times. If he did go somewhere overseas, he might just as readily have gone to the US. He always said that he wanted to chase a hurricane. He'd seen that ridiculous movie *Twister*, you know, with Helen Hunt and Bill Paxton. Awful movie but it just got him hooked. He said he would go to America, go to tornado alley. But it's that kind of dark tourism, isn't it? Those people taking selfies at Auschwitz and Chernobyl. It put him off. He wouldn't feel right about following devastation around, seeing something that kills people, destroys their houses. But he still wanted to go. Was it his fault that they lived where the tornados came, he would say. Would you set up camp on a freeway?'

I waited for a pause. 'How close were Richie and Austin?'

'Austin? What is there to know. They met at uni, started a business. I don't like him, not in the way he has handled the current situation. As far as I'm concerned, he set Richie up, through negligence, or something, I don't know what. Either way, we aren't having any get-togethers in the near future, whether Richie comes home or not.'

If Kim was having an affair with Austin, then her ill-feeling towards him may have come from Austin returning to his wife. Unlikely though, so I tried suitor number two. 'And what about Tommy Clayton. How close was he to Richie?'

The slightest tightening of her lips, the way she brought the glass to them, just quicker than before, hinted that she was rattled. 'Tommy? There is even less to know. He is the dad of one of Emily's friends. A GP. That's all.'

We had only spoken for 30 minutes or so, but it was clear she was getting anxious and not just at the mention of Tommy. 'The girls will be home soon, so maybe we can pick it up again some other time?' It sounded like something Quinn would say.

'Of course. There is always more to discuss, but this has been very helpful.' I didn't want to push and I thought it best that I didn't encounter the eldest daughter again, and give away the secret we shared.

Driving home, past the other big homes on the nearby streets, each worth millions of dollars, I thought about what Kim had said about the lifestyle and the money that Richie had married in to. As far as I could tell, nostalgia doesn't affect one class more than another, or the privileged over the not-so privileged. But what about those who move from one class to another, like Richie had done. What about those from the working class who are future-looking, chasing wealth, and have now found themselves living an upper middle-class lifestyle. Do they long for a time when they had far less, a time before the complications of money and luxury, and the creeping sense of unfulfillment. Having very little could very well be the heart of his happiness, which at the time went unnoticed. Here we find a core of disappointment that nostalgia hollows out for us, the recognition of what was unappreciated.

This is what I understood from the stories my mother tells me. She came from a very large family – five girls, two boys, all in a three-bedroom house, in old Fremantle. A father who was absent much of the time, with very little money and what little money they had was spent on cigarettes and alcohol and cheap vegetables and tough cuts of meat. Home haircuts and hand-me-downs was the norm.

As the children grew older, their fortunes changed proportionally for the better and their children – me and my cousins – grew in number to 40 or more. All of us would congregate for an annual family Christmas picnic at the Fremantle foreshore with my mother and her siblings laughing about, what seemed (to me and their other children anyways), horrific childhoods, telling us kids about how they were so happy, over and over again, each Christmas year, regaling us with the enviable joy of their near-poverty. This is again nostalgia at its most devious. Were they indeed genuinely, without-a-doubt, positively happy; or was this merely the story they liked to tell themselves? Would they go back to those times, we ask. 'Definitely,' they reply, without a second thought. And we are sceptical, knowing how much they enjoy their new prosperity (from which we too have benefitted). Fortunately for them – my mum, aunties, and uncles – time pushes forwards, making it impossible to test their conviction.

Home from Kim's place, I threw myself exhausted into my old recliner. It was about 830pm and the house was in a state of wind down, Maynard in bed, Poochie (our chihuahua) laying puppy-tired in her divot on the lounge. Quinn was watching an SBS documentary on the fall of the Berlin Wall, recumbent on the chaise part of the lounge, warm cup of tea in hand, snug as a bug under the blanket her grandmother knitted for her some 30 years ago, and looking every bit of it, tattered, moth-eaten, only threads holding it together. Other threads had escaped, having been pulled by dog claws and jewellery, and the ends were frayed from being dragged along the floor. This blanket, as old as the tumbling of the Berlin Wall, was a simulacrum of our memories of that day, of the store of our memories. Somewhere, in the worn tapestry of my memory, were fragments of the original news story as it unfolded, on the news, my dad in his armchair, a hard day at work, 1989. I was eleven and the whole event made little sense. An ugly graffitied concrete wall was being hit with sledgehammers. Ordinary people, like us, it seemed, chipping away at it. Quinn and I lived at that time, saw what was happening in an infamous city on the other side of the world, but the world was not ready for us to really see it, to understand the enormity of this moment, its historical import.

Now we were watching the same footage, the same images, but we were older, ready to make sense of it all.

'I can't believe they weren't wearing safety glasses,' I said deliberately.

'That's your take away from this?' Quinn was taking it too seriously to appreciate the fun I was making.

'No, it's just that I wonder how I would act in the same situation. It would really sour the moment if you went blind from sledgehammering. Do you remember me telling you about getting that bullet fragment in my eye from the shooting range, when my pistol misfired? I wouldn't want that to happen again.'

Quinn looked in quiet horror, recognising that I was trying to salvage a crude attempt at humour (which it was) which lead to her thinking of when we first met and then to wondering why one thing had lead to another, the fateful twists and turns, the terrible serendipity, to get to this point.

There wasn't time to properly lament the unfortunate series of events, though, as she was interrupted by Maynard suddenly appearing at the bottom of the stairs. He had been crying and plump tears sat heavy on his plump cheeks, his thin arms and legs sticking out of his pyjamas, elbows and knees like knots on saplings, his teddy bear held firm against his chest. He said to us, as if we were of no kin to him: 'What will happen to me when I grow up and my parents are gone?'

Our hearts broke and real life, here, now, not the past, not the Berlin Wall, slapped us out of its rambling consciousnesses. Quinn held her arms out for him to come to her. She smiled for him, knowingly, as if this were all an important and inevitable rite of passage, I imagine, like a girl getting her first period and suddenly becoming a woman, a boy falling in love for the first time and having his heart broken. A desolate landscape had opened to him, a line drawn in the dirt. No more would he ask questions of mortality – ours, his. He will only have questions of what now, how do I act in light of facts and absolutes.

Maynard went to Quinn, reluctantly, hesitant, almost, to accede to a love that had suddenly betrayed him. I wished for that too, to smile knowingly, and hold my arms out to him, but I could only stare at a spot on the carpet, an unthreaded piece of wool caught on Poochie's claws weeks ago, feeling ashamed that one day I will die, and guilty that Maynard should learn this, come to ask this question, alone in his bedroom, in the dark, with nothing but an inquisitive mind that had stumbled upon this new horizon.

I knew this moment from my own childhood – perhaps every child has the same – when the future was not desirable, not something to run headlong towards, ecstatically reckless, but something to be wary of, kept at a distance, just out of mind. It came only at night, in bed, when sleep didn't take me immediately, a moment when the world of a child can breathe and delve inwardly, make sense of it all. I would lay awake, staring at the galaxy – the glowing decals of moons, and stars, and planets stuck to my bedroom's ceiling – with my brother in his bed next to me, sharing a room, already asleep, snoring lightly. Through reasonable deduction, I learned of their deaths, that my parents will die – they will grow old and the oldest person is only 100 which means they will die before my brother, my sister and I; and this idea of heaven – the place where I will meet them again when I die – was too far away for me, too long to wait. Or, worse, heaven didn't exist; there were only galaxies up there – moons, and stars, and planets, and so much emptiness. Panic would sweep over me, getting hot under the covers, hot and held down by the weight of the duvet, and would need to throw the covers off, with the sudden weightlessness and the blast of cool air calming me. Exhausted from the anguish and somatic stress, I would finally fall asleep and dream of happier things, rainbows and puppies, like my mother told me to do each night as she tucked us in.

Maynard has no brother or sister to cling to in his moments of despair, alone in his room, thinking of our deaths, with only inanimate plush toys for comfort, like the teddy bear he clung to, enfolded along with him in his mother's arms. I asked him to come to me, so that I might hold him tight too, keep his fragility and mine close together, keep each other from breaking. 'Come here, my big boy.' Then, like the myths of Christmas and Easter, I told him false things: 'We will be here for a long time yet. Forever.'

And then I did my best to drag his tiny little mind and body away from the horrors of life into the ignorant, inauthentic bliss of a TV commercial. *Down, down, the prices are down. I still call Australia home.*

We're happy little Vegemites, as bright as bright can be. His tears dried and soon forgot why he came down to begin with.

But I wouldn't forget, and jingles can't hide the facts, arranged like some glum series of syllogisms.

I am getting older.

I am going to die.

I am going to die before him.

Therefore, he is going to be alone when I die.

Seven days until his birthday: Interview with Austin

I slept poorly and woke with a dark cloud about my head, and for an anxious moment felt unclear as to its cause. Like entering a room and forgetting why.

I'm reminded though, at breakfast, by an unsubtle imploration: 'Let's have another baby!' This was not me or Quinn making the suggestion: it was Maynard. I imagine he saw our family like a sidelined basketball team, forever forfeiting games for a lack of players. He was willing the immaculate creation of a companion to combat the loneliness of his soon-to-be dead parents, like Frankenstein creating a bride for his own ungodly creature so that, if they are to be shunned, then at least let them be shunned together. If Maynard's parents are going to die, at least give him someone to mourn with. Others – both friends and strangers – have said, to my face, that a single child is bound for tragedy. Behind their closed doors, we imagine they say worse things: that we are selfish for denying him this; that we denied him this on purpose. They say this as if we were unaware, that it's new information. Stoically, we counter these claims with some half-true, Al Gore righteous bullshit by saying that when it comes to global warming, sustainability begins at home, and that big families are responsible for using up more of the world's resources and polluting it with their excessive consumerism. Or we tell those worried about the arrival of refugees – 'illegals' – coming to our shores to stop having that third or fourth kid which was going to double the population within a generation anyway. And we are concentrating our finances and energy into one child when everything turns to shit. And . . . and . . . and . . .

And yet, this utilitarian logic could never absolve the truth of our selfish hearts which would, without a second thought, fuck all the world to make our only child feel at ease by giving him a brother or sister.

Quinn answered first: 'I'm sorry bubby but we can't have any more babies. And besides, then you would have to share everything with them.'

'That would be okay,' he said quietly, a hint of doubt, still young enough to recognise the sting of having a foe for affection and possessions. Thankfully, that was all as he ran off to the living room, to the TV murmuring away. Quinn and I exchanged sorrowed looks, unable to help him, our bodies impotent from a complicated birth. We could only hope that over time, as he grows, he will be habituated to the reality of our triumvirate family and think on it less and less.

Petal is listening, but again she is fussing with the room, my sheets, pillows, moving chairs about that don't need to be moved. She wants to say something to me.

'Think of that poor boy.' She has very little of her usual gusto when she speaks. 'And look at you, here, hundreds of kilometres away, all broken up like a car wreck.'

There is little I can say or do but accept her reprimand. But I have explained it all before and she has chosen to ignore it. I defend myself anyway, by attacking. 'What can't be helped, must be endured. Isn't that something that you told me when I wanted more morphine for the pain?'

'What's that supposed to mean?' She speaks quietly, like we are sitting alongside each other in a movie theatre, watching the trailers, trying not to disturb those around us, shoving handfuls of buttery popcorn into our mouths immediately after having our say.

'Nothing, but that's where we are, that's where Maynard is. We can't physically gift him a child to beat his loneliness. He will need to endure it.'

'You keep telling yourself this to make you feel better. But I will tell you to your face, it is going to be a difficult life for that boy, especially without you there.'

To this, I don't respond.

And, recognising that she might very well be inflaming the reputed suicidal tendencies of her patient, Petal takes her seat again, smooths out the creases in her scrubs, and folds her hands in her lap. 'Continue, please.'

Having taken Maynard to school early, and hopefully substituted his desire for a brother with schoolwork, recess, and friends, I took some time to stake out Austin's house before our lunch together. I didn't expect him to be home during the day, but it was likely that Jamie – freelance writer and housewife – was. She appeared at about 815am, dressed in a silken bathrobe, waving the three kids goodbye from her doorway as they walked to school. I was unsure if Austin was still home but this riddle was quickly solved, when, just as the children were out of sight and around the corner, a car approached, a black Audi, and parked in their driveway. As soon as it came to a stop, Jamie reappeared, and leaned into the car, driver's side. From where I was parked it was hard to tell who was in the car, but the way she leaned in, the way she let her robe fall open, it looked as though they were very familiar to each other. It was only thirty seconds or more, until she pulled herself out of the car, cinched her robe, looked around the street and trotted back inside, looking back to the car, waving and smiling with a giddiness usually reserved for teenagers. I only had questions: had I gotten lucky, or did this happen every day? Did she want to get caught or just cared little for what her neighbours thought, or that it was no secret at all?

The Audi pulled out and drove by me where I was able to catch a glimpse of the driver. It was a young man, liberal type, slick hair, tan, and wayfarer sunglasses. He was smiling pretty hard to himself too. This added to the complexity of the mystery: it was likely that Jamie was having an affair, which resulted from, or was possibly the cause of, Austin possibly having an affair with his good mate's wife, causing the good mate to suddenly vanish off of the face of the Earth. She hadn't signed the divorce papers and maybe she was reciprocating Austin's infidelity with her own little tryst. Again, it seemed unlikely that Kim and Austin were together. Besides, it all seemed a little clichéd, too simple, too suburban. I was anticipating that our lunchtime meeting might clear up some of these entanglements.

Austin's accounting firm was in the city, a floor somewhere near the top of one of the newer constructions. I caught the train in and headed to about the middle of St George's Terrace. The lobby security meant that he would need to come down to receive me. I waited in a red leather recliner from which I could see the elevator. He exited with two businessmen, clients, walking between them, slightly behind, his hands on their outer shoulders, comforting them. One final gentle slap on their backs and he sent them on their way, before heading over to me. He was much shorter than his profile pictures had suggested. We shook hands – a firm grip but not aggressive. He spoke first: 'This way please,' and showed me to the elevator which we had to ourselves. 'I couldn't find much information about you,' he said, typing in a punch code to access his floor. 'I wanted to check out who it was I was meeting with. I'm sure you understand.'

'Completely. I don't have much info online because of my time as a cop. There's always a criminal out there holding a grudge so it's best to keep a low profile, or, better, no profile at all.'

'What do I call you, then?'

'John will do.'

'Okay, John.'

The lift came to a halt and opened to an open-plan floor with at six or seven desks, mostly occupied with office staff, and three doors to offices towards the rear of the space, and a fourth for a kitchenette. Classical music was playing over the top of hushed chat and keyboard tapping.

I followed him as we walked past his mid-twenty-year-old receptionist who sat at a sparse island desk at the front of the space. 'Shelley, can you bring me and . . . John some coffee please. Latte for me of course and a . . .?' he said, pointing a finger gun at me.

'Flat white, no sugar.'

'Flat white, no sugar, for John,' and shared a wink with Shelley. 'After that, can you bring in our lunch.'

'Yes, Mr Stone.'

We zigzagged past the desks, each face looking to me, trepidatiously. The whole Richie-gone-missing thing clearly had them shook.

'Take a seat, please,' he said, as we entered his office, pointing to one of the armchairs sitting in front of a large dark-wood desk, decked out with a green and gold library lamp and a fountain pen stand – the whole nine yards. There was also a large gold-framed picture of him and his family, holidaying in the snow somewhere. It sat on the desk, curiously facing outwards, towards his visitor, as if to prove to strangers that they did indeed exist. 'You're not the first detective to come calling, although, I gotta say, you do look a little different from the rest. So, how can I help *you*, John, considering there is very little more I can offer?' Austin leaned back in his chair, knitted his eyebrows, and made a tent with his fingers, pressing the tips together.

'You were good friends with Richie, yes?'

'Well, I would say business associates first, friends a distant second. Our wives and daughters were close before we ever were. We had a few similar interests but nothing made us particularly chummy. Most times, if we weren't talking about work, we talked sport and weather. The usual chit-chat.'

'I have these photos from your social pages. I don't mean to pry, but I will have to. You seem close to me,' I said as I handed over printed copies of their families together.

He held each photo close to his face, at eye level, as if determining their authenticity. 'Ah, yes, these are for the business. Part of our PR campaign. Some of these occasions were organised by Jamie,' he said as he threw the photos dismissively onto his desk, as if folding a poker hand, before resetting his hands into the tent.

'I see. Did he ever disclose any concerns he was having, any reasons he might have to take off so suddenly?'

'Nothing I can think of, no.'

'What about financial issues?'

'Damn!' he exclaimed with buoyant sarcasm, 'and I thought we were going to try something a little different today, maybe be a little more creative. Look, I know what you are driving at, and I'm not sure what you've heard but I don't want to tell you anything that the law doesn't already know.' He turned ninety degrees in his chair, looked out of the wall-to-wall, ceiling-to-floor window, towards Fremantle which from that height looked only a stone's throw.

'Fair enough. I get it. Just so you know, Kim contacted me. I'm working for her. I'm not with the police and I am not here to uncover any . . .'

A knock at the door and Shelley came in holding a platter with two coffees and two pieces of sugar-coated shortbread, and placed them in front of us.

'Thank you, Shelley. Can you give us 10 minutes before bringing in our lunch,' he said, turning back to his desk.

'Certainly,' Shelley replied with a warm smile before exiting.

I waited for her to close the door before continuing. 'I'm not digging into anything about your business, nor your personal life,' and gestured with a nod at the family photo.

It wasn't meant to be a threat, veiled or otherwise, and yet Austin took special interest. His little finger tent collapsed, washed away by the onset of a sudden tempest, as he slapped his arms down on the rests, spun towards me, leaned in and made sure I met his blackening gaze. 'My personal life? What the fuck have you got to do with my personal life?'

'Nothing. I just want to find Richie. That's all.'

'That's what we all want. But Richie isn't here in the office, and he sure as hell isn't at my house, so start looking elsewhere instead of wasting their money.'

He let the words linger before reclining back into his chair, turning again to the ocean, fixing his eyes on a freighter standing on the horizon. 'You want to know something about Richie. He was a loser. I felt sorry for him. I'll be straight with you. I didn't meet him through Jamie and Kim. I knew him before, at uni. We studied accounting together. He did fuck-all study, was stoned half the time. Not sure how, but we graduated at the same time and I didn't expect to see him again. And then Jamie tells me she met Kim at a school fundraiser, they got talking, learned that we were both accountants. Work was slow for Richie, and Jamie tells Kim that she will tell me to call him and maybe I will offer him some work. I did, just to keep Jamie off my back, and look at what it's cost me. Inquiries and cops coming out of my arse. They aren't going to find anything, but shit sticks.'

A knock on the door and Shelley entered with another tray but waited at the door, sensing poor timing.

Austin was still searching the flat distant water. 'You'd better get going, John,' he said. 'I have a meeting in five minutes.'

Shelley flashed a quizzical look at him, suggesting a ruse, but the interview was unsalvageable at this point. Still, I thought I might antagonise him a little, test his patience. 'I wouldn't want to ignore the coffee Shelley made for me,' I said as I reached for my cup, took a sip. It was just warm, made for short visits. 'Yummy. What sort of coffee is this?' I asked in Austin's general direction.

'How the fuck should I know? Brazilian? Shelley?'

'Not sure,' she stammered, her head down.

'No bother,' I said. 'By the way, have you heard of the coffee beans that are collected from elephant dung in Thailand? The elephants eat the beans, and when they excrete the beans, the beans are collected and voila – elephant-shit coffee.'

'I thought that was monkeys?' He was suddenly interested, disarmed, looked at me.

'Elephants, too. Maybe you can order some in for my next visit. Expensive though, just so you know. Harder to get than your monkey-shit coffee.'

He laughed heartily, respectful of my audacity. 'I will let you know if I hear anything. Shelley will show you out.'

I skolled what remained of the tepid coffee, but left the shortbread and lunch order waiting on Shelley's platter. Best to leave Austin thinking he still owed me something.

I followed Shelley out, and once the doors were closed asked if I could look into Richie's office. My voice seemed loud as, just as I spoke, all the office-type noises had come to a sudden halt, the faces at the desks again directed at me.

Shelley was caught off guard too. 'I'm not sure if I'm allowed to do that,' she said, looking back towards Austin's office. 'Let me check first.'

I let her call him on the intercom. For a simple yes or no, there was a prolonged and intense discussion, until finally hanging up. 'Let me show you where it is,' she said without a hint of hesitation or duplicity.

And when she opened the door, it was very clear why. The room was all but empty. There was a desk and chair, similar to Austin's, and shelving, but no personal effects, no pictures, not even a computer. They weren't waiting for Richie to show his face. As far as they were concerned, Richie didn't work there anymore.

'When did this happen?'

Shelley folded her arms and looked at her red suede pumps for an answer. 'A few weeks ago, I think. I didn't ask any questions. I am Mr Stone's receptionist, not Mr Curtz's. She was let go on the same day. A temp.'

'When was the last time you saw Mr Curtz?'

'Over two months ago. There was a lot of tension between him and Austin, Mr Stone, I mean. I heard rumours, something about laundering. Do you know anything? I don't want to find another job right now.'

'No, I don't, I'm sorry, but that is why I'm here. Here's my card if you hear anything.'

Shelley took the card, warily, alarmed by the sudden implication, and hurried back to her desk, the light on the intercom flashing urgently. When the elevator closed, the last thing I saw was her on the phone, looking deathly pale.

'It was him that did it, wasn't it,' Petal says excitedly.

'It was him that did what?'

'He killed Richie. Framed, like you said earlier.'

'There is no body or evidence yet to make any such claim.'

'It was him though. No, don't tell me.'

'There's not much to tell.'

'You can tell me.'

'I'm going to.'

'Good. By the way, what is your pain intensity, on a scale from one to ten?'

'Six and steady.'

'Good, good. Continue.'

Six days until his birthday: Interview with Tommy Clayton

The next interview was with Tommy Clayton. When I needed Austin's details, I made sure that I rang Kim to hear her reaction. Very clever of me. However, for some reason, when I needed Tommy's details, I sent Kim a message, which was very stupid of me. I'd shown my hand, which was telling by her very casual response: 'Of course.' Like it was no big deal at all.

He also lived close to Richie and Kim, Austin and Jamie. He was divorced, with shared custody of two boys. He seemed, by all accounts, harmless. General Practitioner at his own practice for the last ten years, member of the PTA, volunteer at the Osborne Park Good Sammy's (a decent drive from his home), campaigned for the local left-leaning female independent. He asked me to meet him at his practice, mid-morning when he took a break before his patient list started to build up.

'Come in, please,' he said, inviting me into his office. He had a warm handshake and smile, late 40s. Smart-casual, with a bit-of-fun yellow SpongeBob SquarePants socks, peeking out from beneath rolled up tan chinos. And a kind face and tall stature that reminded me of *The Big Lebowski*, Jeff Bridges, but tidied up, and with a lot less 'dude'.

'Do take a seat, I only have about five minutes, unfortunately. There have been some doozies already this morning and upset my schedule.' He sat in his chair, spun away from his desk, hands on his knees, waiting for me to divulge what ailed me.

Despite myself, I was charmed. 'Well, firstly, thank you for seeing me. I can appreciate that you are very busy. You have heard about Richie's disappearance.'

'Indeed, it is a real shame. Kim is absolutely distraught.'

'So you've spoken to her?'

'Yes, on the phone, and I have met with her a few times. She was very anxious, hadn't been sleeping well. I do feel especially sorry for the girls. My oldest was in the same class as their youngest. That's how I first met Kim and Richie. From preschool onwards. They, the kids, have moved on to their own schools now, but we have all stayed rather close.'

'I don't want to waste too much of your time: can you think of *any* reason why Richie would disappear?'

'Yes.'

'Yes?'

'Well, it's no secret about the shonky business dealings. I have heard this from Kim, and I assume you have too. And I have heard it from others. It's a well-oiled rumour mill, these private schools. Everyone knows each other's business. But that's all I know on that.

Kim has confided to me on other matters, but I shall keep them private, until Kim tells me differently. Which she hasn't.'

'Can you tell me anything about Richie's health? Was he sick, cancer, high blood pressure, cardiac issues? Anything?'

'Speaking as a GP, I can't really give you any information. However, speaking as a friend, there was most certainly something making him ill. Physically, he was terribly unfit, overweight, which we had spoken about. Mentally, he was very much on edge most of the time. I doubt he would do anything to harm himself, but certainly he needed to find some means of relaxation, meditation, and some prescribed medication. Speaking as a friend, of course,' and tapped his nose, our little secret.

He checked his watch, frowned. 'I will have to get on with my patients, I'm afraid. If there is nothing else?'

'Nothing, no. Thank you for your time. I may be in touch.'

'Is that all!? Is that all you asked him!? You keep talking about Austin, but wasn't Tommy possibly having an affair with Kim? Have you ignored what Smith said already?'

I revel for a moment in Petal's agitation, a sure sign that she is at least somewhat interested in what I have to say. 'I haven't forgotten.'

'Maybe I can put two and two together for you: he's a doctor, she was a physio. Surely their paths crossed at some point before their kids being in the same class.'

'I get your point, but I didn't feel that there was anything there.'
'Feel?'
'Feel.'
'If I was you, I would have asked him a little bit more straightforwardly. "Are you sleeping with Kim; and did Richie find out?" Something like that, maybe.'

'You could be right.'

'I feel like I'm listening to The Bold and the Beautiful, *so you may as well ask the question.'*

'I won't take that as a compliment. More of a 90210 *fan myself anyway.'*

I returned home, and sat heavily at our dining table, with a mug of coffee, packet of double coat Tim-Tams. I had the photos from the shoe box spread out before me, including the hardcopy I had printed out of Richie and his children. There had been no word from Kim about friends emailing though photos of Richie (and I had forgotten to remind her at our last meeting), so, as far as I knew, this was still the last photo of him before his disappearance. This made it important, that it was the last; it would be cherished, either way: first day of school, new beginnings. The type of photo that you *should* print a hardcopy of, keep it safe, protected under the sticky cling film of a photo album, and then, if you have the means, place the albums in a fireproof safe to keep from disaster. How many of us would, without a second thought, run back into a burning house to save our pets and photo albums, comfortable in knowing that everything else can go to ash. At least this was what every bath-robed and slippered interviewee says when the news reporter asks, the camera angled just so to get the smouldering remains of the victim's home in the background. Maybe, today, it would be our smartphones that we risk our lives for, with memory cards full of photos and images. What they have in common – analogue and digital – is that they are the only 'concrete' evidence of our physical existence within the past.

And you must have the photo of our pasts, for posterity. Almost as a matter of principle, as if by not recording this moment you were denying your future self the memories that are being made –

the memories of right here and now. Where are the hardcopies, the digital copies, that prove without doubt that this moment existed and that we were in attendance? If the tone isn't clear, this is our future selves chastising our present selves, jealous of our privilege for having been there. Posterity has a human face – it is ours and it is very disappointed.

Of course, we had done the same – taken photos of Maynard on his first day of school, his first day of school ever – for our posterity. Figurative reels of digital photos were taken, have been taken, to capture the whirlwind of a childhood in still life. Quinn took the morning off so that we could go together as a family, to take him to his classroom and get him settled, each of us holding a hand, his bag on my shoulder, his being too small and slender for the straps to take hold. He didn't look ready, because of his shoulders, and because his school uniform looked far too big for him, even if it were the smallest size they made. Maynard was a small kid, but the uniforms looked large on all the kids his age. Maybe it was an act of compassion by the school, offering these clearly oversized uniforms to ease the distraught, coddling parents into this momentous transition – our babies going off to school for the first time, leaving us to fend for ourselves, but them still looking so small in their big clothes, small enough that they will need us again by the end of the day.

Maynard settled better than I ever did. And where he was brave, Quinn and I were only brave-faced. We walked out of the school gates towards home, our hands reaching for each other's and only when we came to the junction of the street, when we looked each way for traffic, did we reveal ourselves.

'You big baby,' Quinn said with a hypocritical tremor and red-rimmed eyes.

'I know. I'm hopeless. How about coffee at Perk? To debrief.'

'Yes.'

For each it was less a debrief and more a chance for distraction, absently reading a paper, appreciating the warmth and smell of the coffee. Our sadness was selfish. We were not sad for him – he seemed to quickly find some friends, local kids, and was happy for us to leave when the teacher gathered their attention. No, we were sad because something absolute had been lost forever, never to be recovered. We were crying for ourselves, anxious as we were frogmarched towards this new freedom, the long day of emptiness at our house.

We would get over it and our anxieties would soon be redirected. We will cry for him when he fails, when he struggles, when his friends have abandoned him, or he is lost, or when his heart is broken. And then we will cry when we miss his youth, piece by piece, as he gets older and older, the little reminders that take us back to when he filled the house all day and every day. Before school and time took him away. And this will make us cry.

'I have some very sad news for you. They always grow out of you. And you will need to get used to it. My children are grown. We don't cry so much for them anymore, or for ourselves. But Maynard is still a baby so if you need to cry, then do so. It is your right as a parent.'

'I doubt I have much choice in it anyway.'

'That is very true. Now, please, back to the photo. The family photo before school.'

I looked closer at the photo. Having now met Kim, I can say that their girls' faces were perfect amalgams of their parents', but not like most kids, not like our Maynard whose face is best described as a gestalt, a magic-eye puzzle, where my facial features dominate at first, but if you stare long enough, cross your eyes, my face recedes, and Quinn's features take over. Uncross your eyes, blink twice, and my features return. Richie and Kim's girls' faces were instead hemi-spheric, divided by an invisible horizontal line drawn between the top of their lips and the tip of their noses. They had their mother's green eyes, her high cheekbones and pinched nose, but their father's pursed lips and weak chin.

The more I looked at Richie, the more familiar he became. His receding hairline looked just like Scott Weiland's – lead singer of Stone Temple Pilots, circa 1994. A coincidence maybe. Looking closer still, I found more resemblances. I may have been projecting because the chin could have been Layne Staley's or Dave Grohl's, the cheekbones Eddie Vedder's. No, that is too much, no-one has Eddie's cheekbones. What I was certain of though was how Richie's smile resembled Kurt Cobain's, the one he seemed to reserve for interviews, at shows, for appearance, with his teeth clenched, lips drawn wide, the façade of a smile, but the blue eyes intense, a young addict's crow's feet in place of laugh lines. Richie's smile was only a hint of this, but the absence, and the veneer was the same. The look of a man who is elsewhere or nowhere, who walks about in public, humming to himself, his hands locked together behind his back as if proclaiming, 'Don't be alarmed, I won't touch anything, go about your business as usual, just act as if I were not here.' A man of no great influence, careful not to disturb or rearrange the order in which the world about him, a world crafted by those younger than he. A man who is awaiting instruction for what to do next, as if the future were an abject, unyielding amorphous lump of expectation, permeated by the background dread of potentially squandering it. What to do with all this time ahead of me, before it empties indif-ferently into the past. This is the man Kim had described. A loser – this was the man Austin had described.

But this was not the man I am looking for, which is most likely why, at Austin's office and at Tommy's practice, the world remained as it was, familiar and consistent and ordinary. Not like at Kim's, where the familiar and unfamiliar waxed and waned. If I had any kind of insight into the whereabouts of the missing then I would need to trust this 'gift' of mine, where the past calls back to the present. I had a shopping list of leads, more friends and associates from the present and from as far back as the last ten or fifteen years. But I needed to go further back in time and land in the mid-nineties. I needed to meet some of the Scotch boys he boarded with and I would need to find Stevo, his best man. They would know best the Richie I was looking for.

| 2 |

Six days until his birthday: Interview with Damien

It was a poor start. There were very few photos of his boarding days, and Kim was patchy at best about that time in Richie's life herself. She met some at their wedding – Richie had invited them – and pointed them out in their wedding albums but struggled to recall their names. 'Yobbos. That's what I called them. Collectively. A pack of drunken yobbos.'

A perusal of an old Scotch Yearbook did lead me to some names. Aiden, the most handsome of the trio, was in Margaret River and didn't want to be visited, spoken to, messaged, or anything without some kind of warrant. He gave no reason. Chadwick, the happiest-looking of them was dead. Car accident, eight years ago, near Esperance, where he grew up. Richie had attended the funeral. Kim had too, but had forgotten – both his name and the funeral – because 'there had been a lot of funerals that year.'

Damien, the tallest of the three was living in Sydney, and was open to a chat on the phone. I called that night, 730pm Sydney time.

'I'm really shocked by this,' he said, the sounds of a baby crying and a dog barking in the background. 'You've thrown me completely.'

'You haven't stayed in touch with him or anyone who knew him?'

'Can't say I have. We have a lot going on here.'

'Not Aiden, Chadwick?'

'Aiden's lost the plot, and Chad, well, that's a sad story. And now Richie. Feel a bit guilty, to be honest, that I haven't done more . . . well, I'm not sure what I could have done.'

'The good news is that he could still be alive, and there is little to suggest otherwise.'

'But you can't know that for sure.'

'No, I can't. Can I ask you about Richie, at Scotch and the board- ing house. Was he happy?'

'Um, yes and no. Drunk, stoned, with friends definitely happy. School work, heading home, not happy at all. Could be downright miserable actually.'

'Would he ever kill himself?'

'Shit, you don't mess around do you. No, I don't think he would.'

'Would he ever cheat on his wife?'

'Nope, loyal as a hunting dog, and twice as obedient. If you ask me, Kim had him on a pretty short leash anyway. Bit of a bitch her- self if you don't mind me saying. But he wouldn't cheat on her.'

'Would he ever steal?'

For the first time in our conversation, Damien didn't have a response immediate to hand. 'Well, I guess it's been long enough now to come clean, but I do know of him doing a bit of shop- lifting when we were 16, Year 11. Many times, actually. It was after school, or on weekends, in Perth. We'd catch the bus into the city. He never had much money on him because he was a sponsor kid. Which is why I thought he was nicking things. It was always at the bigger shops – Myer's, David Jones, maybe Target if it was there. I can't remember exactly. It was safer in the big ones because there was less staff, fewer eyes watching. One day he just started pocket- ing things, small things but they weren't cheap. Bottles of perfume, neck ties, books, kitchen stuff, like garlic presses, salt and pepper shakers, action figures from the toy department. One or two items at a time. He didn't need any of it and never kept it. Most of the time 'Saint' Richie – which is what we started to call him – would leave it at the feet of a homeless person at the train station. But that didn't really help the homeless in any way so he started taking what he stole back to the store, usually a day or two later, different cashiers on if possible, and invent some sob story about how it was a gift but it was the wrong size, colour, style. Or he said it was a mothers' day present he'd bought for his mum but she already had that perfume, or she was allergic to it. Or he would say that his retarded baby brother (who didn't exist of course) might choke on the small parts that came with the action figure. He'd say to the poor girl at the counter: "You wouldn't want that to happen, would you? He's already suffered enough don't you think." When they asked about the receipt, he'd just say that the same baby brother tore it up, or the dog ate it – the one that they had to put down because of a twisted bowel or something – he got that from *The Simpsons*. Next thing he's walking out with a pocket full of money and a smile from ear to ear. What a shithead. But Saint Richie would redeem himself by giving most of what he had to the homeless guy and save just enough to treat us to Hungry Jacks. We never really thought he needed a reason to do what he was doing but when I did ask him, he said he was giving the middle finger to capitalism. We thought he was a bit of a hypocrite though when he's saying that with a Whopper, fries and Coke in front of him. I reckon it was more the thrill, getting a kick out of almost being caught, that really made him do it.'

In the background, the cry of the baby was getting louder.

'Anyway, to cut a long story short, he did it for about six months until he got nabbed. We were out the door, about to make our run for it, and then this security guard got hold of him. Me and Chad took off. He didn't dob us in, though. Not that we had anything on us anyway. There was no prosecution but he did get sent home for a bit. That's about all, really.'

It was more than enough and I hung up feeling pretty good about it having learned a little more of his character: not only was he a lazy, nihilistic Che Guevara but an adrenaline-junkie hypocrite of a Saint – Saint Richie.

'I remember when my son got caught stealing. He was twelve. He stole a pack of mints. Fishermen's Friend, I think it was. Horrible things. He started bawling his eyes out and said how he didn't even like them. Me and Roy laughed so hard. We grounded him for a week, which really meant something back then. And we made him eat every last one.'

'I can't imagine my Maynard stealing anything.'

'There is something of the devil in little boys, and I hate to say it but just about every one of them has the potential, even if it's just a smidge.'

'Not my Maynard.'

Petal held her tongue but couldn't help grin at my arrogance, as if telepathically projecting into my future a triumphant 'I told you so' for when it is revealed that my sweet, darling boy is indeed a cute-looking skin-sack of slugs and snails and puppy dog tails.

Five days until his birthday: Interview with Charles; Third meeting with Kim

My next step was to get out of Perth, follow the trail to Richie's past – to Manjimup and the farm. I planned to head there the following day. Before that I needed to have another meeting with Kim. She had texted me, saying she'd found something I might be interested in and should come by that night. I didn't want to waste any time so I took the opportunity to take the day to visit Richie's father, Charles. Charlie, they called him, in his seventies, weak-chinned, white-snowy-haired, and, as Kim had said, in the early stages of dementia. It was time to take the trip to Mandurah and see what Richie's old man could still remember.

For the journey down, I chose Alice in Chain's *Dirt*, a quintessential grunge album, heavy, angry, at times melodious, a tour de force for the ills of drug abuse. It was just under an hour long which was almost the exact time it would take to get to Mandurah. There hadn't been any reason for me to head that way in years, not since the new Forrest highway was built which meant you could bypass it altogether, and even before then you could take the South West highway. Our family had holidayed there once when we were kids. It was a small town then, not the sprawling city it has become. It must have been '85 or '86, summer school holidays, and if ever the heat was at its most reckoning, it was when it was beating down on the roof of our already-old 1975 white HJ Kingswood as it rolled down the highway. The five of us in the steel trap, with no aircon and vinyl seats, the kind that made you sweat and your skin stick fast, so that every now and then you had to peel the underside of your thighs away. The Kingswood also had the metal seat belt buckles which became hot as a stove top if caught by the sun. We copped our fair share of burns, shirtless as we were after a swim at the pool or at Cottesloe beach. On the longer holiday drives, we would always arrive exhausted and dishevelled, pools of sweat running down our backs and into arse cracks. It didn't help having the three of us kids rolling around on the rear bench seat, sick with boredom and pent-up frustrations. Always my sister in the middle, my brother on the left of her and me on the right, some unofficial seating arrangement established who knows when. Sis was supposedly the mediator, the buffer, between the boys, but she couldn't help get herself involved, pinching us with her long pink-polished fingernails (thank *you*, *Dolly* magazine), delighting in drawing blood and yelps from her younger brothers.

The bottom half of the Kwinana freeway didn't exist back then; you had to take Stock Road, then Rockingham Road, and finally Mandurah Road. It was a much longer drive too, lots of traffic lights, indirect routes through Kardinya, Spearwood, Coogee, Kwinana, Rockingham and then on to Mandurah. It was a bleak drive, taking you past everything that was unattractive about the outskirts of the city: the Kwinana industrial area, the Naval Base bus depot, the stunted vegetation of a coastal highway, and acres of hobby-sized vege patches. There were also the stockyards and tanneries just north of Kwinana, since been moved elsewhere. Because of the heat, we had the windows down, trying to catch the breeze, but frantically wound them up again as the smell of rotting meat and sheep shit filled the car. Still, it found its way through the gaps of the Kingswood, seeping through the door seals, the vents, threatening to suffocate us all. We held our breath as best we could until it passed, all the while my brother, sister and I wondering of the nature of their business.

But then, amongst what seemed a wasteland, was Bibra Lake.

'There it is', my brother exclaimed. 'There's Adventure World,' and unbuckled himself so that he could half hang out of the car window, pointing skyward, towards the top of a steep embankment, at the canopy that sat above the speed slide, my sister and I craning our necks to get just a glimpse of the greatest place in Perth.

We stayed in a chalet at one of the original caravan parks in Mandurah, some of which are still there. It was older Mandurah, close to both the beach and to the estuary which divides old Mandurah from the newer canal suburbs which at the time belonged only in the imagination. The nearby coast was bordered with fibro houses, beach shacks, seaside shanties, with lawns that were brown or weed-ridden for a good part of the year for the sea salt air, which also did little for the paint work on the weatherboard and rusting gutters.

At the caravan park, my sister read books, whilst my younger brother and I wandered freely, exploring where we liked. Nearby, between the older houses, were abandoned blocks, long vacant, for decades, as if contaminated, or held in bureaucratic holding patterns, red-taped. Most had long weeds and unusable dirt mixed with construction waste, devaluing the more well-maintained houses on either side. Some of the vacant blocks had trees, gumtrees, tall and sturdy in their branches which we climbed immediately, as if it were the most obvious thing to do. All the way to the top, fearless, thumbing our nose at death, like you could in those days. Like a ute-full of teenagers driving a 100 kay down a country road, or an ashtray full of cigarettes, smoked to the filter and then some.

We wandered further to a dry gully nearby, overgrown with wild scrub, except for the remnants of a concreted road or carpark which was cracked into haphazard slabs allowing thick wild buffalo grass to come through. There were high grey Super 6 fences of houses that backed onto the gully, falling towards it, the ground beneath steadily eroding away. On the bank was a rusted car, burnt out, windowless, the fluffy white lining of the bald deteriorating tyres peeking through. There was still enough of the car seats and steering wheel for us to sit in the shell, act like we were driving, peering over what was once a dashboard. There was no roof or doors which gave the feeling of being open and safe from the dark and the places of spiders and snakes. Our parents' warnings ringing in our ears always: be wary of snakes and strangers. Sound advice, but our parents, in need of a break themselves, weren't concerned enough to not let us go by ourselves, eight and six years old as we were then. We made growling noises for the engine, pretending to turn the immovable steering wheel. In that car sits two skinny lumps of innocence, whimsy, and wonder. But, as I look at them from afar, they seem childish. They are children, but look every bit too old to be childish. Maybe it is because I doubt Maynard and his school friends would make these same sounds, touched as they are by a techno-induced jadedness that makes them seem far more savvy and streetwise than my brother and I ever were. Even so, there is no chance that we would let Maynard go anywhere by himself. Snakes and strangers everywhere.

It was a quiet hidden space, with the high fences, seemingly avoided by adults and children alike, as if it were cursed instead of enchanted. It was school holidays so we expected the streets and every other available public space to be teeming with kids. We listened for their voices but heard none, and decided to break the silence by throwing gravel at a cricket-ball-sized hole near the top one of the fences, testing our aim, given it was cricket season. Neither of us had a good arm so the gravel cracked against the fence and some flew over the top into the hidden back yard. We were good boys, kept our noses clean, and for us this mischief-making might have been considered unusual behaviour, which is why we were so startled when a woman's head popped over the fence and started yelling at us. Our immediate reaction was to hide behind some thin bushes, and shut our eyes, which was about as successful as if we had pretended to faint and prostrate ourselves in a feeble attempt to play dead.

'I can see you,' the woman said to the conspicuous pair of idiots. 'Did you hear me? I can see you.'

We heard her, but cowered vigilantly, unwilling to acknowledge the matter-of-factness of her accusation.

She called out again: 'I am waiting for an apology.' But she quickly grew tired of it all and left us with a weary reprimand: 'Don't do it again, or I'll tell your mum.'

Only when we were certain she had gone did we spring from our hiding spots and sprint all the way back to the caravan park, thriving on the pain in our chest, the taste of blood in our mouths, and stopped only when we were back at the chalet, doubled over, out of breath, both unnerved and exhilarated, having crossed a line from good boys to bad. It was temporary though, a fleeting dalliance with the devil, with neither of us really growing a taste for it ever again.

It is from this place, this experience, the intensity of this moment as children, that a memory was created. Because of its wonder and its destabilisation of the balance of our young lives, an intrusion into our characters. Because of its secretiveness, unseen as it was by our parents. A place just for children to hide and play. Thirty years on from what was a mere week in my lifetime, it has stuck, held fast, repeating itself. But like so many memories, it wasn't plucked from thin air. It was beckoned, as I made my way into the old part of town, the same way we came all that time ago, intensifying with each recollection, building familiarity, feeding the nostalgia, beckoning me to find it again.

Which is why, having arrived an hour before visiting hours, I went looking for this place again, not knowing whether it still existed, and, if it did, I wanted to see how well my memories had held up against the past. I drove slowly, finding my way at first through my Google navigation and then by feel. There are more buildings and developments, and a marina has sprung up nearby, but I soon found the road leading to the gully. It was almost as if nothing had changed, still overgrown and abandoned, truly a haunted place. I parked where the bitumen was still a road, and where grass runs along cracks like monstrous caterpillars, just at the edge where the red gravel beneath the black spilled out on to beach-white sand. Some of the fences had been replaced, newer, sheet-metal and painted, but serving the same purpose of keeping this blighted place hidden from their eye line. Surely bodies were buried there.

Just out of sight from the road, nestled in the overgrowth, was a two-person dome tent. I must have disturbed the occupant as the tent's fly zipped open. I was half-thinking that Richie was going to pop his head out, that he'd gone off grid, possibly in Mandurah, possibly to be closer to his father. Instead, it was the head of an ancient-looking man. He stooped as he stepped out, and remained so as he looked around, poked at unseen items hidden in the high weeds that moated the tent. He spotted me, met my eyes, waited for me to react, but when I didn't, carried on indifferently, leaving me feeling ashamed, having invaded his privacy in this very public space.

I left the gully, back on the road, which is when I saw another sign, this one pointing in the direction of the Mandurah Greyhound track, beckoning a second memory from that same holiday. My parents weren't gamblers as far as I could tell, although us kids had spent some time hanging outside a TAB. It must have been a big occasion because the then Prime Minister Bob Hawke was going to be there. I hadn't a clue who he was, but my father told me he was very famous and was the leader of Australia. This was no small detail as I'd begun to develop a child's sense of nationalistic belonging – I was an Australian and from what I could tell, that was a good thing – and a newfound understanding of my place in the world, my allegiances, my colours, the green and gold, all of which were made material in a growing collection of Australiana: an Aussie-themed place mat, Australian flags, boxing kangaroo and koala plush toys. And here was our great leader, plonked in a backwater town, watching lean dogs, like men, chase false hope.

'You should get his autograph,' my father said, not just because it was Bob Hawke but because that's what you did when others had decided that someone was famous.

'I might shake his hand instead,' I said disobediently, and walked right up to him, finding a way through what was a thin crowd, as if his appearance here, middy of beer in hand, was not so unusual. Straight up to him with uncharacteristic confidence, that of a patriot, maybe. It was a warm and gentle hand that held mine, a twinkle in the eye and a strong voice. 'Good on you, young fella,' he said with a wink, as if he knew, like no one else did, that my loyalty was true.

There is no photo of this moment. No autograph for my archive. Just that memory. But I can reveal that I invented what Hawke said to me. He did say something – that is true – just as the truth of what he said is out 'there' in the universe's infinite memory for those things we forget. I can't remember the words and know for certain that they will never be retrieved, but I can also tell you that the year of our holiday was different too – a plot hole in my own story – as a bit of research would suggest that I was much younger than I thought. The only explanation was that we'd made an earlier second trip to Mandurah, and the two fragments of these memories had been woven into one. It is absolute truth that is always responsible for challenging the integrity of our memories, proving that we likely have been self-deceiving ourselves all along. And it is this self-deception that perpetuates these untruths, gives impetus and incentive to our longing for something that never really existed. This is the impetus of the missing. And I must remind you that this trip to Mandurah was only one week in my life, one out of nearly 2000. I never lived there and hadn't been back until my visit to Richie's father. And, yet, this is where you might find me, if for some reason you were ever looking.

The retirement home where Charles stayed was much as you would expect: cream walls, pastel flourishes, a safe, blue herringbone patterned carpet for wear and tear and spills and fluids. On the walls in the reception was a triptych of printed artworks, of harbour views, looking out from the shore, towards a grey ocean with various sized sail ships. In the first of the series, the ships were setting sail, full spinnakers heading away from shore, whereas in the second the ships were returning. The final was of three or four ships, washed ashore as if after a storm, beached, de-sailed, unmasted, impotent, waiting for the tide and a fresh gust of wind that the solid teak picture frame will never allow. A grosser metaphor I've never seen.

Parked up in the halls were wheelchairs with sleeping inmates, at peace, at their leisure, moored, for themselves; others, wandering with aimless purpose. It is easy to quickly lose your sense of humour. Truly places of looking back, returning, and of no return.

This was only my second visit to a home in as many years. My grandmother, in her eighties, had finally made the transition. I had Maynard with me, four or five years old, her great grandson. He was fawned over by the staff and residents, the spirit of youth in his smile. My grandmother, though, wasn't making any attempt to hide her anger and shame, declaring openly that she didn't belong with these people. 'Don't get old,' she advised. This was the second last thing she ever said to me. A month later, on her death bed, surrounded by me, my mother and father, sister and brother, uncles and aunties and cousins, she said the very last thing: 'I don't want to die.' She said it without any of the wisdom or grace that I'd expected of the dying. There was only a discomfiting terror in her eyes. 'I don't want to die,' she repeated, staring deeply into our eyes, looking for reassurance that she wasn't dying, and clutching at each of us, rubbing our hands, as if they were lanterns housing genies. But she was dying and she did die and left behind very little other than an affirmation of our mortal fears.

I was shown to Charlie's room by a tall male nurse, whose tattoos and demeanour suggested that he could likely moonlight as a bouncer. 'He can get aggressive, when he gets confused. We do our best to just let him believe what he wants to believe. And here he is.'

In a small room in a small chair was a frail seventy-something man, that could hardly beat the dust out of his own shirt, let alone assault someone with any conviction. Despite the overwhelming mugginess of the room, he was enveloped by a brown cardigan, and brown slippers which poked out from under a CWA knitted blanket, rainbow coloured.

'This is . . . sorry I have forgotten your name,' the nurse said by way of apology.

'That's okay. It's John.'

'Who's this, then?' Charles said warily.

'I have come to have a little chat, about your son, Richie,' I said, drawing an armchair close.

'Richie? Haven't seen him in a while.'

'I was hoping you could tell me a bit about him, when he was younger in Manjimup, the places he liked to play, his best friends.'

'Why?'

It was a good question. I had to think on my feet. 'Well, it's his fortieth birthday soon and I was hoping I could tell some stories about his childhood.'

'And who exactly are you to come asking questions?'

'I'm a friend, from Perth. Kim said I should talk to you.'

'Kim sent you? Couldn't come herself, eh?'

'Unfortunately, she is very busy.'

'Bullshit. No one's that busy,' he said, agitated, but seemed to enjoy having someone to be agitated with. 'What did you want to know other than him being too soft to work a farm, and too much of a city-boy snob to visit his father.'

'Why do you think that is?'

'Eh?'

'Never mind. Can you tell me a bit about his childhood and teenage years. Who he hung out with.'

'I don't know. He was always on his motorbike around the farm. Or when he was littler we'd drop him town to his mate's place. We caught him roaming around with these two boys. They were playing video games, in this kind of dungeon attached to the deli in town. Lots of older boys there. Smoking. Swearing. I guess that's all part of growing up.

'One of his mates was Asian, Vietnamese. I fought in Vietnam you know. But that's not something we were proud of then. But I helped people like him and his family.' He paused, remembering what I had asked, an enthusiastic jolt when he did. 'The other boy is fair-haired, tall and skinny. He was going to be the next Bruce Reid, bowling for Australia. By Jeezus he was quick. Even when he was little he had the ball swinging all over the shop.'

I jotted down the notes as I listened.

'What are you writing? Let me see that,' his mood changing quickly again.

'Nothing, really.' I held up the Moleskin for him to see but his reading glasses were elsewhere and he waved it away derisively.

'I prefer football myself. Not today's footy though. Too soft. A game for girls, now. Richie has two girls. Maybe they're going to play,' he said frowning. 'You got kids?'

'Just the one'.

'Just like Richie.'

'He was an only child wasn't he?'

'He never was happy about it. My wife was pregnant with another but he was born "still" as they say. She was never the same after. We waited too long you see. It's a shame. Strange that in the end he had one boy himself.'

'I'm not sure what you mean.' I had with me the photo of Richie and his girls and held it up for him to see, to remind him of what he'd just said moments ago. 'You say he had a son, but in this photo . . .'

He lashed out, snatching the photo from my hand. 'Don't contradict me you piece of shit. Richie didn't have any sisters. It was just him.'

'My apologies.'

He nodded an acceptance, and, by way of an apology himself, handed the photo back to me. We both sat silently. I waited, confused. He was staring at the door behind me, as if he'd heard someone knock. 'I hope my Richie has some children one day. He is an only child. He needs to build a family. Maybe with that girl he's been seeing.'

By then I was struggling to keep up. 'Does Richie have a girlfriend?'

'Ha! He's too shy for a girlfriend. Scared of girls. He likes the prettiest ones though. He can't look them in the eye. I think he thinks he isn't good enough for them. He even blushes when he says the word "love." He is a romantic, I guess. Or a sissy. He just needs to concentrate on school anyway. Girls will only get in the way.' The sudden levity seemed to get his body moving, his pointed knees, hidden beneath the rainbow blanket, began jumping up and down.

'He should have a girlfriend. He's good looking and clever enough. Just like myself. The apple doesn't fall far from the tree. Lucky he has some of his mother's good nature, though. She's an orange, I reckon. Me and Richie, we're apples. He's good natured but he has been hanging around with some never-do-wells.'

Without flinching, Charles farted gently. 'Looks like it's time to pay the ferryman,' he said matter-of-factly, and threw the blanket off and made his way to the en suite.

I wasn't sure as to what I was meant to do – rude to leave or rude to stay – but thought best to use the time to process the information.

The mention of the deli was interesting. We had something similar near to where we grew up. A double-storey, brick-and-tile home with the bottom floor dedicated to the deli, the upper floor for the residence. A garage to the side held five or so arcade machines and one pinball machine, the carpet black with decades' worth of grime, and gum, and ash.

Can you see it?

It was the early '90s. Arcade machines like Mortal Kombat, Street Fighter, Raiden, The Simpsons, and even maybe an older machine with 1942, Wonder Boy or Ghosts and Goblins. The pinball would also be *The Simpsons*-themed or maybe Schwarzenegger-themed, *Terminator 2*, or *Predator*. Can you also see a boy standing next to one of the machines, watching on as a bigger boy plays. The little boy is just above eye-level with the controls, which are being assaulted by the teen. He watches the game longingly, as if, by waiting there long enough, one of the older boys will shout him a pity game. The boy feels that he would do well, that he could complete the game easily. He has watched the older boys play for hours and hours. He knows when to run, when to stop, when to jump, when to shoot, to bomb, block, punch, kick, duck. If only he had the forty cents to play, then he would show them how it's done. And then he could put his three initials in the top players' leader board, amongst previous victors. His name would look good alongside 'FUK', 'DIK', 'COK', 'NOB', and 'VAG' – each of them legends of the game.

Can you see the blue cigarette smoke as it gathers near the low ceiling. There are a few older boys and a few older, older boys there. Richie is twelve, but on the young side still. There is a NO SMOKING sign and every now and again the owner comes out to the garage and tells them to put their cigarettes out; but the same owner also stoops down to collect the coffee can on the floor, full of butts, empty it and return it. The older boys have long hair, and stink of cigarettes and body odour. Richie would come home stinking of fags. His mother and father would know that he wasn't smoking. He had no money besides, and they were babies really.

Can you see the little ones wearing their primary school outfits, the older boys in their high-school uniforms, and the late teens wearing jeans, and black t-shirts. They wear desert boots and their voices are broken, deep and loud, and they punch and kick each other for fun, or spit on the machine when the game comes to an end, the foamy ooze running slowly down the screen, just missing the coins which are lined up on the rim at the bottom of the screen. The dormant pinball machine wakes up with beeps and pings and recites quotes from the film it's based on. *Hasta la vista, Baby.* Lights flash and it goes back to sleep.

Can you also see the little ones running into the deli to buy lollies. Teeth, bananas, chicos, jelly babies, milk bottles, strawberries and cream, spearmint leaves, raspberries were all two cents. Cobbers were three cents. Spend your money wisely when making your choice. Money which came from recycling one-litre glass coke bottles at the same deli. Cokes tastes better in glass. The young ones push a converted pram to exchange the bottles, fifteen cents each. Maybe even look beyond the two and three-cent counter to the Double-Dip sherbet, a packet of Fags (later rebadged as 'Fads'), Big Boss Cigars, hand over the hard-gotten gains and the circle was complete.

Richie's father retuned from the toilet, draped his blanket over his bouncing legs, and picked up some thread of a conversation. 'I remember watching the '70 grand final, Carlton versus Collingwood, 120,000 people they estimate. Carlton were 44 points down but came back to beat the Pies. It was on the TV, black and white. I remember the commentator screaming "Jesaulenko, you beauty." There was all the streamers and paper that covered the oval and the stands.' Charles chuckled to himself. And then became serious, exhaled through his nose, before speaking again, all the exuberance of the story gone. 'That's what I see when I look around at this place. We're like streamers, scraps of people, blown around, when the game's over. If you don't mind me gettin' poetic, we're like a ticker-tape parade on an empty street.'

His legs had stopped bouncing, and like a wind-up toy at the end of its spring, he seemed to shut down, leaning forward slightly, hands on his knees and stared at the floor. It seemed well timed as the head nurse was at the door and clearly unhappy that a stranger, detective or not, was over-stimulating her patients. 'Time's up, I'm afraid.'

Her voice startled Charles awake, something left in him, a last gasp. 'Yeah. And bring me back a Chiko roll from the deli would you Richie. That always gets me through.'

I looked to the nurse for help. 'Will do.'

She nodded a begrudging approval but was already wearying of the charade.

'Thank you, Mr . . . but visiting hours are over.'

We left Charles falling asleep in his chair, and she walked me to the front sliding door. 'He forgets soon enough about these plans. Other than a few incidents, he doesn't push or make a fuss. He just seems to return to his crosswords, sudoku, Scrabble and jigsaws. He's happiest when he is doing these things. Why are you here, if you don't mind me asking?'

'A family matter.'

'Shouldn't there be other members of the family here. Ones with power of attorney maybe?'

'Next time I will bring someone to verify.'

'Please do.'

'Can I ask if his son visits at all?'

'Not recently, no. But that is none of my business even if it is yours.'

She then swiped a card attached to the lanyard around her neck to let me out, and with the air of a mafioso matriarch, turned her back and returned to an office some ways down the herringboned corridor.

I drove home with an uneasy cloud about my head. The feeling that something was wrong in the world, something that I was unaware of and unprepared for, which is why I chose something sombre to listen to for the car trip, Alice in Chain's Unplugged album. Beautifully dark songs, the wonderful harmonising of Layne and Jerry Cantrell, rivalling Lennon and McCartney, or Simon and Garfunkel. It was Layne's return from a hiatus, looking balled up and thin, like old newspaper used for packing delicate things. My favourites were 'Nutshell', 'Brother', 'Down in a Hole.' And 'Rooster,' Jerry Cantrell's tribute to his Vietnam Veteran father. I thought of Richie as I listened. What is it like for a son to see his father's mind begin to deteriorate right before his eyes, bit by bit, losing a grasp on the present and its connection with what came before. To no longer recognise his father, and no longer be recognised by his father.

Something else was troubling me. I had been reading pop-anthropologists, listening to podcasts, blogs and they were all saying that this new generation – collectively gen alpha, the first to be entirely born in the twenty first-century – might also be the first to live very long lives, or even be the first to live immortally, which is, after all, the unspoken goal of humanity. I was reminded of what Maynard had said only a few nights before. Maynard could very well be one of the last children to see his parents die of old age. And when we die, we will never see each other again. My body, and the consciousness housed within, will have dispersed into nothingness and I will no longer bear any relation to him or him to me, our ashes scattered. Like the remnant litter of Charles' ticket-tape parade. Orphaned and anonymous to him, strangers, with no familial history. No kin to him. If only I could lie to him and to myself of God and heaven and immortality, only then could we be content, holding onto the small flickering flame, knowing that we will again meet some day. Willing to make the most of it, heaven and God, a warming jingle, to make life and our mortality fade into the background of our anxious minds, forgetting that we must make the most of it because one day it will be gone.

I had spiralled, at 100 kilometres an hour on the freeway. Sensibly, I put the indicator on and pulled over in the emergency lane, parked the car, and wept.

When I picked Maynard up from school that afternoon, I squeezed him until he asked me to stop.

Petal is shaking her head, just a slight show of concern, and sucking air through her teeth. 'You need to get those thoughts out of your head. This negativity, death, suicide. I'm beginning to wonder what you have said is true about your fall. What state of mind you were really in. And you might just need to find yourself some kind of religion to give you a little more hope about what's still to come. You don't have to be Christian, although I would recommend it. You can be Muslim, Buddhist whatever you like as long as it keeps your eyes heavenward, even if that heaven is up or outside or inside. Heaven can be anywhere and everywhere, I guess, but it is hope that all of these kinds of worships have in common.

'Keep going, now I've had my say.'

I wanted to stay home that night: tuck Maynard in, bedtime story, hot chocolate, go to bed early with a good book, and sleep for ten hours or more. Contrary to the accusations made by Kim and Petal against their husbands, I did look at myself in the mirror on occasion, and what I saw was the dark circles under my eyes, the pallid tone of my skin and the return of my old acne rash raging red on my forehead.

But I couldn't miss my meeting with Kim. She had again arranged for the girls to be out. And, again, she looked different when I arrived, but familiar, too, as she looked a lot like me: pale, washed out, purple bags under her eyes. Her hair was twisted up in a messy bun and was dressed in baggy grey sweatpants and matching hoodie. There was no hip hop playing. No beverage offer. She just walked me directly to the dining table and took a seat. On the table, a wine glass, half-empty, with the near-empty bottle waiting nearby. And a small pink envelope, gilded on its edges, with long flowing gold script on the front which read 'To Richie.'

'I went through the shoe box before I gave it to you,' she said flatly. 'I don't feel bad about it as I was looking for something, some hint, like you were trying to find some hint.' She paused, looking for my eyes, for me to acknowledge the purity of her motives. I did with a slight nod. 'I took something that you won't have seen. I wasn't trying to hide anything. I was just angry and hurt.'

She picked up the envelope and gently pulled out the letter from inside, and held it, the delicate paper trembling like a flame between her fingertips. 'I've done nothing wrong.'

'No, of course not.'

'I read it. Only a few days ago. I had to. It's a love letter, from some girl called Debbie. It's dated December 15, 1994.'

She placed the letter in front of me, and stared at it a moment before reaching for the bottle, which I took as a sign to pick it up. I unfolded it as carefully as if it were a mummy's wrappings. The paper, A5, faint-ruled, was soft and the two fold-lines – in half and half again – had worn thin and fibrous, just ready for a little hole to appear at the single intersection. So easy to tear in a fit of heart-break, or betrayal, but it wasn't. Just read and folded and unfolded and read. There was a polaroid attached by a blue paperclip of a teenage girl. My first impression was that she looked like Lisa Loeb from the 1994 song *Stay*. The librarian glasses and dark lip-stick. She was the girl from the other photo, the girl sitting on the wall, watching him as he danced. In this new photo, her smile was pressed closed, lips thin, embarrassed, although the corners of her mouth and her eyes showed that she was happy, giggly, a little shy, flattered. Boys weren't immediately drawn to her and nobody went out of their way to tell her she was pretty. But she was. Her smile. Richie had told her.

> Dear Richie,
> I was so happy to receive your letter. I didn't think you would write at all. The last two weeks were the most wonderful of my life. You are such a great kisser, ha ha! I probably shouldn't write that but who cares. Those lyrics for 'Lover you should have come over' are so beautiful. I think I am in love with Jeff Buckley. I would like to think it is me he is singing to. Not really. I like to think that it is you who is singing to me. I can't wait to see you in Perth. I am so excited to be moving away. Imagine us, Perth locals. I need to go now but know that I love you (not as much as Jeff Buckley though, ha ha!)
> xx Debbie

I folded the letter up with even greater care, knowing now its gravity, and placed it on the table.

Kim stared at it, and, without looking up, spoke the same. 'Have you ever felt that kind of love?'

'I'd like to think I have.'

'So did I. But a long time ago. Before Richie, when I was a girl about her age. It is stupid to be jealous of someone from twenty years ago, of someone else that felt this way about Richie and that maybe he felt the same about her. I can't compete with her. I can't compete with that kind of love.'

'Do you know Debbie?' I asked, but Kim was elsewhere.

'He used to say that "Lover you should have come over" was our song. He said to me that Jeff Buckley was saying what he wanted to say. That he didn't have the words or the music, but it captured what he felt and thought. About being too old and too young at the same time. That he could be blind, and that he needed to "awaken". He wanted to sing what Jeff Buckley was singing, and he wanted me to be the girl that he imagined Jeff Buckley was singing to. And just like Debbie, I wanted to be the girl that Jeff Buckley was singing to, and the girl that Richie was singing to. But I wonder, now, if we weren't all just imagining someone else.'

I let the silence that followed hold the air, to speak for the sad quavering truth that lay as bold and tangible as the sheet of paper in front of us.

Only when Kim reached for her glass did I repeat my question from earlier. 'Do you know Debbie?'

'No, but Stevo might.'

'Richie's best man at your wedding. The one in the photo with him.'

'Yes. You should talk to him. He might know where you can find her. And I guess when you find her you might just find Richie too.'

Kim gave me Stevo's details, and I rang him as soon as I was home. I told him about Richie, and that I was going to come down tomorrow to meet with him. Like Tommy, he was shocked but happy to help. He still lived near Manjimup. I booked a motel in

Manjimup online, packed a small suitcase, took care of some school admin, and at close to midnight fell immediately into a deep sleep, and was woken only when Maynard was beside our bed again, but this wasn't about breakfast.

'Where are my Hulk gloves?'

'He has been rummaging through toy boxes and bookshelves since you left last night,' Quinn said from the bathroom.

'Where are your what?' I asked.

'My Hulk gloves. The ones Uncle Brad gave me for my birthday.'

I maintained a calm demeanour but inside I was reeling. Something had changed. 'Don't you mean your Hulk *glubs?*'

'Yeah, my Hulk gloves.'

Since he was gifted the gloves over two years ago, Maynard had been mispronouncing 'glove,' instead saying 'glub.' It was cute for a while, and Quinn and I would share a laugh, but were also at pains for him to say it properly, reciting for him the proper way, correcting him over and over again. And suddenly, as sure as midnight ceases one day and begins the next, what we had hoped would come, had come, and what was, was now the past. And it was not at all what I had hoped for. I wanted to correct him again, tell him that it is *glubs*, *glubs* and should always be *glubs*. This is what I wanted to say, and hold him by his arms, bring his face close to mine, to show how important this was. I didn't and, sour as it tasted, I praised him instead, knowing that this was only the start. Soon, instead of the innocent lyricism of 'Daddy' or 'Da da', he will refer to me as 'Dad' – shortened, mono-syllabic, blunt. I wanted to tell him to wait. That he was leaving without me, leaving me behind. I was not ready. And his indifference, his ignorance of the milestone, told me that it wasn't up to him or me. His journey was not my journey, no matter how functionally integral to his journey I might be: I provide, I comfort, I advise, but our histories, intertwined as they are, cannot be the same, or run at the same pace, his story in ascension, mine in declension. Just like when I kiss him on his perfectly plump cheek, I cannot get under that perfect skin and become him, squeeze our bodies together through love in a way of keeping him from change. This tiny overcoming of a pronunciation issue left me wrought, in the throes of what was a second panic attack in as many days. ['Breathe', Petal tells me, 'In and out. You are escalating.']

I told myself I must breathe.

'Breathe', Petal tells me, again. 'In through the nose . . . and . . . out through the mouth.'

I do as she says, but it is hard to breathe with cracked ribs, no matter how shallow, how little I allow the bones around my lungs to move. Here on the ward, busted leg, busted ribs, trying not to suck much in at a time. We take a breath between 12 and 20 times a minute. I am taking shorter, more frequent breaths, about 25 per minute, 1500 per hour. A little sting of pain each time on top of everywhere else that hurt.

That is except when the procession of morphine begins, which Petal tells me I am due for. The process itself is calming. She brings in the needle on the little kidney-shaped plastic tray. She walks slowly, a steady gait. Cautious. She places the tray on the side table. Asks me to roll over as best as I can onto my side so that she can stick it into the fatty cheek of my arse. Rubs an alcohol swab on the injection site. Takes up the needle. Removes the cap. A prick. She pushes down the plunger, slow, and then it's one long long long breath into oblivion, with the faintest, fading echo of my voice speaking the words: 'I love you, Petal.'

That was the first few times, but now I fight to stay awake (or is it tolerance), so that I can enjoy the sensation. And despite the sense of calm that I know is coming, I can feel my heartbeat elevate as she goes through

the process. The fresh needle, machined, sharp, the scientifically manufac-
tured drug, FDA approved. And then I feel myself falling deeper into the
pillow, into my bed. I lay there, stretched out into my prone, elongated
form, straight armed and legged (the unbroken one), stiff and still as a
plank on a jetty, worried that if I move just one muscle I might disrupt
the trajectory of the liquid coursing up through fat veins, straight to my
brain, worried that it will be slowed by the baffles of my body, that it will
instead dissipate into my flesh, before it reaches the brain; be absorbed
elsewhere where it has no use. It has its effect on the brain, not the body. All
the mess of my busted-up body remains, but the alarm bells are silenced.
I think of this as I lay prone, watching Petal dispose of the needle in the
yellow sharps container, watching only with my eyes, no movement of my
head as if my spine were fused. I watch her again take her seat, book in
hand, making herself comfortable, knowing that right now I have no way
of doing myself harm. Right now, I am as weak as a kitten, and just as
threatening.

Four days until his birthday: Manjimup; Interview with Stevo

It was time to head south, to Manjimup. I packed the car, got
Maynard off to school, and organised my playlist for what would
be a good three to four-hour journey. I decided on Soundgarden's
Superunknown, Faith No More's *Angel Dust,* and Stone Temple
Pilots' *Purple.*

The way to Manjimup was along the South West highway which
makes its way through other little towns, Donnybrook, Bridgetown.
Along the road were brown wasteland pastures, huddled sheep,

huddled cows, dams hardly filled. A tough life, one I never envied. The solitude was not for me. I had heard of country hospitality and how wonderful it can be knowing everyone in a small town, but TV, film and novels suggested that this was a gothic myth and the reality was something like *Wake in Fright.*

I'd planned to stay at the motel at the southern outskirts of Manjimup, which, just like Mandurah, I wasn't a complete stranger to. My grandfather once lived around there, moved down from the city when he had grown too old and unwieldy to live with his wife of thirty years. He was a drunk then, as he was most of his life. Everyone I met, during my stay and, later, at his funeral, kept telling me about how intelligent he was but he'd made some poor choices along the way and so here he is, dead at 65, killed too young by old age and alcoholism. For these reasons, my father never drank and discouraged us also, fearing that there was something in us, some genetic flaw, that wanted to take to the bottle with such gusto, lurking in us like cancer cells waiting to be activated. I was never a big drinker either – because of my father's concerns – and even when I did have a beer, it was with a bunch of other beer-snobs, our conversations littered with wanky brewer's jargon.

My father knew that his father didn't have long to live so he sent me to make what was likely to be a final visit, just to remind me that I had another grandfather, or to remind his father that he was a grandfather also. I went in the school holidays, just about to turn fifteen. An old mate of my grandfather's owned a vineyard. I took the bus to Manjimup, the first time without my brother or sister. (I wonder now why they weren't there. Why me? I wasn't any closer to my grandfather than my siblings). When I arrived at the bus depot, my grandfather, to his credit, was waiting. He wore an old cheap grey cardigan, dark blue slacks, and thin Surfer Joe thongs, giving everyone a good view of his horny, yellow toenails. That and the grey stubble on his loose jowls, the receding thin grey hair, made him look far older than the 60-odd years he'd lived so far. The dark expression on his jaundiced face told me he was being put out, as if the raising of kids and their spawn had long passed him by; pissed off that decisions he'd made decades ago were back to haunt him.

For all I knew, there might have been a heart of gold buried under all the gruff and polyester; maybe living with him for the week, and the drives to and from the vineyard, would rekindle our acquaintance. This wasn't to be: no sooner had I put my luggage in the boot of his old white Sigma, did he drive me to the farm, where he left me for the duration of my stay. Whatever my father hoped for didn't eventuate, or it was my father's way of saying 'I told you so' if I were ever to ask about why I never saw him. He wasn't the best father for my father and he wasn't going to start being the model grandfather either.

The only thing he did say to me as we drove to the vineyard was that he was doing me a favour, and 'You had better not let my mate down. So listen up, pay attention, do what he tells ya.'

He hadn't said anything before this, so I took it to be meaningful advice. 'I won't let you down,' I said to him as if he had gone out on some precarious limb to get me this week-long seasonal job, getting paid a third of what an adult would make, even if I only did about half as good a job.

I reckon I was grateful for it in the end, just because I didn't have to stay with him. Picking grapes was simple enough. There were two crops of grapes: one for wine and the other for table grapes. My job was to trim away the dead grapes, the mouldy ones, and pack them carefully so as not to rub the precious bloom off. The wine grapes were far easier: just cut the bunches of grapes off the vines and throw them straight into the large bins in preparation for processing, mould and bugs and rot, a detail they asked me to keep to myself.

It was me and a gang of backpackers, American girls, late teens/ early twenties, just too old for me, but not too young for them to flirt with me, and try to get me to blush. My work suffered because of it and it wasn't long before the owner moved me to another section.

I spent my nights in an old caravan from the sixties, a good fifty metres from the farmhouse, stranded on blocks, its adventuring days long behind it. It wasn't much protection against the cold winter nights, and I had to rely on exhaustion to keep me warm. In the caravan I made my breakfast of toast, using an old toaster that folded down from the centre exposing the red-hot springs that browned the thick leaves of fresh farm-baked bread. At lunch there was more bread and local ham and horseradish mustard that near choked me to death, having spread it thick like strawberry jam. I washed it down with strong Earl grey tea from a tea-cosied ceramic pot, which took time to get used to.

At nights, alone in the caravan, there was a copy of Joseph Heller's *Catch-22*, which I read only because there was no TV. And as I read, I would laugh out loud into the darkness beyond the lonely-standing caravan. Yossarian's life was absurd; war was absurd; and this moment in my life, this life of picking grapes, was absurd.

Which is to say it wasn't for me, and I never expected to return to Manjimup, to visit my grandfather or pick grapes, and yet, twenty-five-odd years later, there I was, again, Friday night, in the same pub where my grandpa may have once drunk, and I may well have been standing in his same place, sitting on his stool, ripped vinyl, and exposed yellow stuffing. Long gone he was and is, so no chance of bumping into each other.

There were six or so men there, locals, at ease after a long working week, and no women. Rolled cigarette smoke lingered in the woolly jumpers and coats of the men, who would step outside into the cold, one at a time, to light up. It was colder there than the city, and chimney smoke blanketed the town.

I was nursing my second middy of Victoria Bitter, fedora on the bar, when I got a tap on the shoulder.

'Doctor?' I looked around to see a much older face than the picture Kim had given me from their wedding, even if I had added the fifteen or so years of aging to it. But his clear blue eyes were unmistakable. He had a full beard and his blonde hair was cut short. Still tall, but thick like a man in the country is supposed to be. Blundstone boots, blue jeans and a red flannelette shirt, worn appropriately, functionally, with the sleeves rolled, not folded, above the elbow.

'Yes, Steven is it?'

'Yeah, mate. Stevo will do.'

We shook hands, his lumpy fingers crushing mine like he was using blunt pliers to cut fencing wire. All I could offer by way of comparison was the stubborn callous on my retired trigger finger.

'Good to meet you. Thought the pub might be an easy place to meet.'

'Better than any.'

'I was going to order some food.'

'I could eat. The steaks are huge. Come from a mate's farm near Ferguson Valley so should throw a bit of support his way, I guess.'

It could have been awkward, two blokes dining together, and Stevo did look a bit uneasy when we first sat down, at a booth, which made it extra cosy, but I made sure I had my notepad out, jotting things down to indicate the situation was for information gathering and not a date. We ordered steaks with chips and had two more beers brought to the booth, shifting gear from middies to pints, full strength, which seemed unsensible given our ages.

The dim lighting exaggerated the acne pock marks on what could still be seen of his cheeks. He wasn't nervous, and yet he struggled to sit still, always looking for someone he might know. Maybe he was just hungry as when the meal finally came, he hunched over the table and sawed away at his steak, greedily throwing chunks into his mouth whilst also feeling compelled to speak. 'So, you're a doctor, eh? But not the real doctor, you know what I mean, a GP?'

'That's right. It's different, study for almost as long though.'

'Yeah right, but you don't cure anyone?'

'Not exactly, no.'

Stevo forked another lump of rare steak into his mouth, chewing through his words. 'I was Richie's best man. We'd known each other for years. He went to boarding school only for a year, nine months really. But, I tell ya, he had changed a lot by the time he came back. Would have been 1993, year 10. He just seemed to have switched off, like the lights had gone out. He was kicked out of the boarding house for shoplifting and maybe smoking weed. So his parents brought him back to the farm. He was moody all the time too. I guess we all were a bit. There wasn't much to do and not much to look forward to growing up here. Didn't help that we started getting on the piss on the regular. Just getting smashed on the weekends. Year 11 was a fucking mess. But he was smart and he got through it and straightened himself up for Y12, when he went back up to the boarding school. Had a year off and then left for Perth and uni to study finance or something. It was a strange choice. Could have taken over the farm, no worries at all. The succession was all in place. Broke his father's heart, four generations it was. His only son turning his back on his legacy. That was what his father kept saying: it's your legacy. They enrolled him at the Bunbury Agricultural School. But he didn't want to go to Bunbury – had his sights set on Perth. His folks eventually let him go. They had come to a compromise but without really telling each other why they made the compromise. His father let him go, hoping that it would satisfy his need to leave but hoped that Richie would ultimately return as a "resource" – someone to figure out how to keep up with the changing market. They could get labourers in but they needed him to look after the books, sort out the taxes, all that +stuff. But Richie went to the city knowing that his father was using him, which is why he did what he did.'

'And you were close with him this whole time?'

'Definitely, in Manji anyway. I think he found some friends at the boarding school and he was catching up with them again when he moved back up. After that we hadn't spoken much, the occasional message, and then, out of the blue, 2003 I reckon it was, he rang me up and asked if I would be his best man for his wedding. I hadn't even met Kim yet.'

'And since then?'

'Hardly a peep.'

'It's meant to be his fortieth next weekend. Saturday night. He was having a party. I take it you weren't invited?'

'I knew it was coming – his is exactly a fortnight before mine – but first I've heard of a party,' and shrugged his shoulders almost happy not to know. He looked as if he wouldn't fit with Richie's new crowd anyway, and it was also possible that Kim had only invited his work friends or her friends.

'Another?' I asked, pointing to his empty pint.

'Yep, I can call in late tomorrow so why the hell not. Let one of the kids run it,' and lifted his half-filled pint to his bearded mouth and knocked it back in a gulp.

I was already swaying, bringing the beers to the table, and knew I had to quickly push through my questions. 'Did he have many girlfriends when he was here?'

'Nah, he was always too pissed. He was a good-looking guy and had girls after him, but he couldn't talk to them when he wasn't pissed, and when he was pissed he was chatty for an hour and then passed out. Besides there weren't many girls here to start with. We knew those at school but we didn't meet anyone new coming to town. Slim pickings.'

'I have a picture of someone, not sure if you know her.' I held up the picture, which brought a grin to his face.

'Oh yeah, that's Debbie. She was from Pemberton but caught the bus to Manji for high school. I don't really think of her as a girl-friend of Richie's as such. They were together for a few months. He left and she stayed. He met Kim not long after and "boom," they were married, had kids, and acted like Manji and Debbie never existed.'

'Where is she now?'

'Not sure.'

Before I could ask a follow up question, two men, mates of Stevo and dressed in the same fashion, came over to the booth. We had finished our meals, except for the decoration of salad, and decided to move around the corner where we watched the second half of the football, played some unflattering games of pool, and had a few punts at the TAB hidden to the side, all to the tune of AC/DC, INXS, Cold Chisel and the odd Slim Dusty. I also listened to stories that had been told many times before, but could be replayed less for my benefit, and more for theirs. It was all recent history, none that featured Richie, who was long gone for the city. I asked questions when I had the chance, trying to swing the conversation my way. I also wrote some of the responses in my Moleskin, none of which seemed useful, intelligible or legible by the end of the night. By the time 'Drinks' was called at closing I found myself stumbling onto the street, under hard streetlights, and with very little to brace myself against the cold. I remember that Stevo must have said something of a goodbye to me but he was already gone. The motel was too close to catch a taxi but too far for the walk to be pleasant. But I also knew that I wouldn't be able to lay down in the state I was in, and anything but sleeping could only have a positive effect on how

I'd feel tomorrow. I needed to walk. maybe even try to jog, get the blood or oxygen or liver or whatever working to purge the booze from my system, burn the alcohol off, like pouring wine into a frying pan.

About halfway was a playground which was a good place to have a break. The orange streetlights kept the main road lit but the park was shrouded in darkness, either to save power or keep the riff raff from congregating. Nevertheless, there were four teens hanging around the swings. I kept my distance, quietened my step and sat on a bench nearby, which I needed, something to steady me, regain my composure for the rest of the journey home. By their voices I could tell that they were two boys and two girls, and by the way they spoke I could guess that there was an established couple (a boy and girl), speaking familiarly and at ease with each other; that the other two weren't together was evident by their exaggerated gestures and the playful teasing. I also guessed that the couple had convinced two of their respective best friends to join them in the hope of fixing them up. The scheme was both philanthropic and utilitarian: philanthropic because the couple didn't want their friends to be lonely; utilitarian because if and when their friends' conversation stagnated, the girls could talk easily together, the boys could talk easily together, and at the end of the night they had several options as to whom will leave with whom. The boys were pushing their respective girls higher and higher on the swings. The girls would scream with every push to affirm their girlishness for the boys; and the boys, to affirm their boyishness, responded by laughing and pushing them even higher.

I felt ill from the thought of swinging, not wanting to watch, but also scared to close my eyes because of the pokie-like spinning that began as soon as I brought the lids down. They were drunk too, the girls especially. They had come over to the swings in the dark, safely hidden from small-country-town eyes, and I imagined had tossed their shared bottle of bourbon – Southern Comfort for the sweet taste, or vodka which was better for mixing – to the side, giddy already from drink and hormonal nervousness. I imagined that this was likely their first time back to the playground since the day they had outgrown it. One day, some years before, like a flick of a switch, the idea of the playground, the joy that it offered, had become dark in their minds, a room they no longer need enter. Years passed and they, now very much changed, were back at the playground for the first time since the last time; back to where they could act like children again, free, immature, even as they engaged in grown-up things, like drink and sex. It was their first time back to the playground and also quite possibly their first experience of nostalgia. But not how you or I might know it, not in the eyes of those who have aged, had kids themselves. These children – for that's what they still were – were still looking forward, to their futures, fool-hardily as it may be, recklessly, but were concurrently very aware that, for them, it was still possible, still acceptable, to venture back to the past, freely, without judgement. Old enough to have grown out of child's play, but young enough to backslide momentarily, which, unlike those of us tormented by nostalgia, does not hurt in the gut nor does it create the desire to dwell in this new-old place.

There is an undeclared age for when the nostalgia for things of our childhood becomes less acceptable. I don't want to necessarily throw Quinn under the bus, but in our early days of dating, I had attempted to 'cure' Quinn of this affliction, which sounds terrible when said out loud, like cults trying to cure homosexuality. We were at one of the shopping malls in the city, and passed one of those games/pop culture stores, Granny May's or Gamesworld, filled with all kinds of objects from the quaint to the kitsch. In the shop window was a twelve-inch-high Astro boy figurine.

'I love Astro boy,' Quinn said, smiling in the way that made her eyes squint cutely and reminded me always of why I had pursued her so doggedly.

'What do you mean you *love* Astro boy?'

'I love Astro boy. I used to watch it all the time when I was a kid.'

'So did I. But I *loved* Astro boy. Past tense. You *loved* Astro boy. How would you describe your feelings now?'

Eye roll. 'Please don't. I love it. Present tense.'

'I don't think so. Given the chance, I doubt you would binge watch all of the old episodes of *Astro boy*. I think you love the *idea* of Astro boy and how much you loved it. You have seen a figurine of Astro boy – something cherished from your childhood that you had forgotten about – and it has brought back warm memories. That is all. You *loved* Astro Boy. Past tense.'

'Fuck you. Okay, I *loved* Astro boy when I was a kid. Happy?'

I wasn't and she wasn't, which is why what they had – those kids at the Manjimup playground – was something to envy: their connection to their childhoods, and the pure joy it brings, can be excused for its sincerity; and because the elastic band that binds the present and the past will remain supple for a little longer at least, where *love* has not yet become *loved*. Something for us to envy, but for these children it is certain to be overlooked, because of hormones and hangovers. And only when decades pass will they see themselves as I saw them, and be envious.

I left them at the swings, careful not to draw attention and make them uneasy by perverting their fun. If discovered, they might laugh at me, poke fun at the drunk, or the boys might assail me to assert their role of protective boyfriend.

They didn't see me, or chose to let me be, but as I walked home, I did hear laughter. Just as I heard it at Richie's home in that first visit. The buildings' facades shifted into something unfamiliar but the overall sensation was the familiarity of something echoing from my past. I tried to place the feeling, searched for it, but I couldn't think straight for the laughter coming from the left of me, unseen, as if behind fences, and, as always, there was the threat of my calling out. But it didn't come, the laughter died, and the surrounds re-emerged from their shadows. I stumbled my way back to the motel, walking in the middle of the quiet street, to avoid falling into the deep gutters, and because of an intense desire for open space.

Three days until his birthday: Meeting Sarah; The farm; Camping

That was the last thing I remembered when I woke the next morning to a mild sun easing its way through thin drapes, sur-rounded by strange walls. I was also fully clothed, on the floor beside the bed, laying face first in a saucer-sized pool of blood. I stayed prone, played dead, listening for movement, but could only hear the harmless sounds of local traffic. And given that the blood was cold and had soaked to a partial sticky crust on the carpet, the attack – if I had been attacked – must have happened some hours ago. If they wanted me dead, then they had plenty of time to get it done.

I let a few minutes pass before easing myself up from the carpet and sat with my back against the bed, letting the scene sink in. A quick scan of the room found no evidence of a ransacking: my wallet, keys, phone, were all there, on the side table near the door. I also found that the door was locked from the inside, which was curi-ous in itself, given that the assailant would have had to consciously twist the latch on the knob when they exited, instead of just getting the hell out of there. Outside, there was also no evidence of a blood trail leading to my room or out of it.

The bathroom mirror confirmed a blunt force trauma just above my right eyebrow. Which also didn't make sense. Why attack from the front? Why take the chance of being recognised if you weren't going to go the whole way? Was this a warning? Was I being told to stop looking? And by whom? Was it one of the boys from the park? But why pass up the possibility of 'getting some' to sock some bloke that was already at home. I was certain it wasn't Stevo or anyone from the pub. I hadn't offended anyone as far as I could tell, sticking to gentle sledging during the pool games and talking non-committedly about football and the weather, whilst also avoiding politics, religion and art altogether. Besides, the last thing I do remember Stevo saying was that he was picking me up from the motel sometime in the day to go camping, and that if I wanted to know more about Richie then I would have to see the farm and the place where he almost died. This of course had intrigued me, and was underlined several times in my notebook which also, thankfully, hadn't been taken.

Even so, I thought it was just pissy talk; that was until I heard a ute roll up right outside my motel room. It was eleven in the morning which either meant I had been unconscious for up to ten hours or just really needed a good sleep that only alcohol or a blow to the head can bring about.

I let Stevo in and was hit by a cloud of Old Spice which almost made me heave whatever remained in my stomach.

'You ready?' he asked, somewhat impatiently, as if I were his wife still putting on makeup before a night out. He then spotted the gash on my forehead. 'Faark, what happened to you?'

'Not entirely sure yet.'

'You okay?'

'Not sure of that either. I think maybe I am but there's a bloody riot going on in my head. Or maybe a circus.'

'That explains why this place smells like elephant shit.'

'Did you know that in Thailand . . .'

'Huh?'

'Nothing. You're early, aren't you?'

'Yeah, I thought I'd better check in on ya. You were looking pretty smashed by the end of the night, had the wobbly boot on.'

'You don't know the half of it. I'm not feeling up to much just yet.'

'Too early to head out anyway. How about you clean yourself up a bit, make yourself presentable, then we'll grab you a feed, and find someone pretty to fix up that eye.'

Stevo threw himself into the ute and started it up. On my side I was greeted with a lolling tongue – another kelpie, the same red as Kim's, standing in the ute's tray. It could have been the same bloodline, they were so close. Unlike Kim's lazy-bones, Stevo's Kelpie stood to attention, its body lean its eyes focussed, ready to work.

We drove only a few hundred metres up the street to one of the bakeries, the kind that has a reliability that you can't dream of outside of a McDonald's. The same pasties, the same pies as far back as I can remember. I ordered a potato pie and a finger bun, a can of Coke to accompany the pie, and a flat white to go with the finger bun. Calories for days. The hiss coming from the oversized coffee machine – the new addition to the bakery's line-up to satisfy the wants of tourists more than that of the locals – had a soothing effect, whereas the pie and Coke (and some Panadol) only sparked an angina fire.

As I sat and ate at the little round tables outside the bakery, Stevo yarned with the baker over the counter, probably fielding questions about what happened to the outsider outside with the bloodied noggin. I felt exposed as I ate, watching every car go by and every person walking the street. Eyes seemed to follow me without looking, like I was the titular character in *The Truman Show*. None of it made any real sense. I only felt comfortable when we were back in the ute, and moving.

The someone pretty that would fix up my eye just happened to be Stevo's ex-wife and she wasn't exactly a doctor and more the local vet. I wasn't in any kind of mood to remonstrate about her credentials and felt equally thankful and embarrassed at the kind treatment being offered.

We walked into the reception area which was empty of people and animals, but full all the same with the smell of urine and shit and wet animal and disinfectant. Everything wanted me to be sick.

'Sarah there?' Stevo asked the young girl at the counter, barely seventeen but likely one of the few people in the town available on a Saturday morning, even if she did look vaguely similar to one of the girls from last night on the swings.

'You know she is. Her car's right there, in the carpark,' she replied with poorly veiled animosity; most likely the gossip surrounding Sarah and Stevo's broken relationship had been a little lopsided to Sarah's take on things, which is not to say it wasn't accurate.

'Hey, Sarah,' Stevo yelled to the back rooms. 'Can you fix this city boy up for me? Can't hold his liquor, as you can see.'

A small woman, dark hair, dark eyes, reminding me of an *Alien: Resurrection*-era Winona Ryder, complete with pixie cut and space-suit (her grey scrubs), emerged, rubbing her hands with sanitiser. 'You trying to wake up my patients or what?'

'Sorry, I'm feeling a bit deaf today. The pub got a little rowdy as you can imagine on a Friday night when the boys are in town and got a thirst on.'

'The boys, eh? *Your* boy has been pretty rowdy too, lately.'

'Anything specific or the usual?'

'The usual is enough.'

'I'll come around tomorrow arvo, have a word with 'im. We'll talk too. Cuppa tea and a scone. My treat. Anyway, can you fix this fella up.'

She had glanced at me only the once the whole time he spoke as if she were used to strays being brought in by well-meaning idiots. This time she looked at me a little closer, scrunched up her nose and eyes, still rubbing her hands together. 'I can do humans but they complain a hell of a lot more than cows and horses.'

'Not this one, tame as a milking cow at sunrise.' With this he winked at me, the butt of his banter which also seemed strangely like flirting with his ex-wife.

'Bring him out back.'

I imagined she had a loaded 12-guage for the look of hope-lessness she wore. But she stitched my eye gently, with tenderness, her cool, disinfected hands touching my forehead, her eyes close to mine, which met every now and again, in an accidental brush with intimacy. Stevo stayed out front, annoying the poor girl on reception some more.

'How'd this happen then?' Sarah asked as she dragged the thread of the first stitch.

I winced involuntarily, which went unacknowledged. 'Not en-tirely sure.'

'Been drinking though?'

'Yeah,' I said as if she were my mother stating a fact which also established culpability. 'At the pub.'

'Steven will do that to you,' she said pulling the second stitch through. 'You're looking for Richie, aren't you?'

'That's right. Do you know anything about it?'

'Just what Steven has told me. Which is not much. I never met him and hardly heard his name when we were together. Me and Steven, I mean.'

She finished, an underwhelming three stitches, brought a small pair of stainless-steel scissors up close and snipped the tail of the black thread. 'All done,' she said and stood back to admire her work.

'I appreciate it. What do I owe you?'

'Nothing. Besides, a friend of Steven's needs to save everything he's got.' She then gave a wan smile and patted me on the shoulder, sorry for me and herself.

From the reception came Stevo's booming voice. 'I got a call to take care of something. The new kid has fucked up the bailer. You want a lift?'

I was loathe to holler back, but felt compelled. 'I'll find my way, thanks.'

'Cool. I will grab you this arvo. See you babe.'

Sarah rolled her eyes. 'He does that just to piss me off.'

'Thanks again.'

'No worries at all. I hope you find him.'

'We all do.'

I left Sarah's clinic feeling only a little more together. The paranoia remained, but with less intensity, which was why I was willing to walk the few kilometres back to the motel. It also gave me a chance to take in more of the surrounds of Richie's hometown, and think on what it meant to have left the town you grew up in, the place where most of your formative memories – good and bad – are made. His last years here, on and off, were from when he was in years 11 and 12, which, as Kim had said, were somewhat of a disaster. Kicked out of the boarding house, sent back home, and then back up to the boarding house with a second chance. In between, he was home for holidays. In between, he also met Debbie.

I looked for the places where he would have caught up with Debbie, away from the prying eyes of parents. There are more intensities in our hometowns than any other, concentrated as they are within the imagined boundaries. If he had come back here, he could probably draw a map of how and where they fell in love: here is where we first met, at the school oval, a Saturday night, with all of my friends and yours. This is where we first kissed and awkwardly banged our teeth together, because we didn't know how; me trying to kiss like I thought you were supposed to but I was too enthusiastic and you told me to slow down. This is the little jewellery store that I took you to, where I tried to impress you by buying you something special with the few dollars I'd saved. You liked jade so I found some earrings with jade in them and you said you loved them. This is where we went for a fancy dinner, at the expensive restaurant, French it was, gone now. Never had a chance. You didn't have the right kind of dress for something so *la de da* and you were nervous because it was very serious and maybe we were getting serious, even if we were only seventeen and had only been together a few weeks. This is where I pushed you on the swings and where we laid on the grass and tried to talk like couples should, like we see couples do in pictures of Paris, talking about hopes and dreams. But it didn't quite work and we ran out of things to say. So we just stared at the stars, and made fun of our friends.

With you, in your room when your parents were out, we sat together on the bed and I could run my fingers through your long auburn hair, and twist it into pony tails, and you would sit there with a slight smile, red lipstick, that I never liked to kiss because it was so sticky. We would listen to love songs and break up songs, The Cranberries' 'Linger,' Jeff Buckley's 'Last Goodbye,' 'Lisa Loeb's Stay.' You looked like Lisa Loeb, which made me want to hold on to you even tighter, not wanting to be the guy in the song, telling you, falsely, to stay. You said that I could never be that guy, just as you adjusted your turtle-shell spectacles, which seemed to give your hand away, knowing that I could, I would, indeed be that guy;

as if you could predict my future better than me. You knew, better than me, that I would be selfish, but you would put up with it, just enough, and hope that tomorrow I would change despite the world being so determined. You would ask me to stay. Knowing that I wouldn't.

'You sound like you have had this very clear in your mind, maybe you are speaking from experience?' Petal says.

'Maybe some of it, not all. Some comes from books, films and TV. This is the Richie I imagine. That's what I do: imagine; imagine and intensify. I can't help but think of how brutal a first love and a first breakup would be in a small town, where everywhere you turn within its small circle reminds you of your past and a feeling, an emotion, associated with those agonising memories. Why go home. Why go home to that place of heartbreak.'

Stevo picked me up a few hours later from the motel, having fixed the issue and threatened to sack his farmhand. 'Fuckin' kid will not listen,' he said, shaking his head, wondering if it was too late to fire him for real. 'If he wasn't the local copper's son, he'd be out on his arse.' He breathed out of his nose for a long exhale, stroked wisely his bearded chin. 'Well, not much I can do about it now. I guess I can take you out to Richie's farm.'

'I can follow you there. I've got my car.'

'And a handsome Cruiser it is but I'm not letting you behind any wheel, not with a possible concussion. Vet's orders.' (Sarah must have said something.) 'And what sort of a host would I be anyway. You ready?'

I packed most of what I had into my travel case and left the car at the motel which was booked for another night. It wasn't too far to get to the farm, a half-hour's drive. We drove with the windows down, taking in the cool air, the noise of the diesel engine broken only by the dog going spare when another vehicle came the other way, or when a flock of sheep ignored her.

'Here we are,' Stevo said, pulling wildly off the road and stopping just short of a gate, his bullbar almost taking out a milk-can letter box, which had uncollected mail spilling from its spout. Near it, a wood-and-tin lean-to shelter, the type that are dotted along the road for the school kids waiting for the bus. I can see Richie, the child from the photos, sitting on the hard, rough-cut jarrah planks, alone. In winter, the rain falling on the corrugated tin roof, rain on tin. It would have been cold, not much shelter from the wind. Maynard wouldn't last a second, either blown away by the wind, or turned into a popsicle, what with him looking more like a marathon runner at home on the hot Kenyan plains. I couldn't live out there either, hayfeverish all the time, blood noses from picking the dirty dry snot. Too weak for the land. I know that for sure. Not these folk though. Born tough. Or maybe just bred tough. If it wasn't the former, then they would have their work cut out breaking some unfortunate kid in.

The lock on the gate was cut. Bolt cutters. Fresh, too; clean. A Lockwood padlock. Could easily have been the unknown lock to Richie's key, which was no good left in the city, sitting in a shoebox next to duck-down doonas. No good if you wanted to come home.

Stevo swung the gate open, and the kelpie, which was out of the ute before it had even come to a stop, sprinted off, familiarising herself with all the dogs and their piss that came before her.

We drove up the long dirt driveway, some hundred metres or so, the homestead at the end, which stood out on flat laser-levelled land (if I remember my schooling). Richie still owned the farm, every bit of it in his name, but it hadn't been worked in a long time. There were no crops, sheep, or cows and the grass that was there had been burnt, bushfire or otherwise. Red dirt too, cracked patches where troughs of mud had once been, despite the season, as if the rain had all but bypassed this lot. There were a few dams, with puddles of mud in their base.

The dirt drive merged into blue-metal near the house. Stevo cut the engine, unbuckled his seatbelt, but remained behind the wheel. 'I'll let you poke around. Give me a yell if you have any questions.'

There had been a few houses on the lot – three generations of them, like family. The newer main house looked in fair condition. It was rendered yellow brick, with a tin roof. A pile of wood rested against the length of its side. Grey and dry and old.

Behind it, hidden from the road, was a weatherboard house, half the size of the newer house, its windows smashed, and had no path to take you there easily.

The only evidence of the earliest third house was the blackened bricks of a lone chimney that stood proud against the landscape. A bushfire maybe had claimed the rest. Up close, the mortar between the coarse, homemade bricks was thin, and in spots you could see right through. A strong gust of wind was all it would take to bring it down. There had been plenty of wind, though, and the stubborn fireplace had withstood it all.

Beyond the house were four sheds, the size for a tractor, or whatever they liked to keep in them. Again, some were old, in a state of slow-motion collapse, and some were new, the galvanised Colourbond glistening in the cool autumnal sunlight.

I looked at the main house first, and checked the door, which was locked. The back door was locked too but a window for the main bedroom had been pried open by a flat-head screwdriver, evidenced by a touch of scuffing and a squared depression in the wood frame, as well as flecks of paint where the hinges had been disrupted, forced up and out. It had been jammed closed again, but my knife did the job and it swung open easily. I waited outside a whole minute, listening, feeling the pulse of the wound above my eye, rubbed the stitches which felt tight and strong; and encouraged, I hopped the sill. It was dark, except for a few blades of light coming through skylights, and from the doorway leading out of the room, which I followed, trying light switches as I went and finding none working. For the first time since I left the force, I wished I had a gun on me – not just my Swiss Army knife, with its five-centimetre blade, can opener, tweezers, and toothpick.

The doorway opened to a kitchen and dining area and I was reminded of images I had seen of Chernobyl, the homes left by the evacuees. Rotting dinners still on plates, washing on lines, TVs were running when they left, or so I'd heard. This farmhouse was the same, abandoned in a hurry. A home that was lived in one day, and then, in a blink, the living were gone, as if vaporised, atomised. Except that, on the kitchen counter, was a stocking of oranges, with a Woolworths tag on it, half a loaf of bread, an open bag of potato chips, can of Coke. How long ago had someone been here? By the state of the rotting fruit, and the rainbow mould on the bread, it could have been within the last month. I think of my stay at the vineyard, and me and Stevo eating his mate's steaks at the pub. No farmer would buy supermarket fruit or bread unless they were absolutely desperate. Richie might have though, because, as far as I could gather, he was no farmer.

The question comes again: Why come home? Why return if this wasn't for him, a 'life on the land'? Had he seen that he had made a mistake, running away from it? Was it a desire to return to honest work, labour, purpose? The admirable work of the farm. And it is noble to feed others, to provide a need. Accounting, worming out tax returns, gaming the system, could hardly compare.

'Really? What was it: he wanted to return to the labour and purpose of hard work?' Petal has become extremely animated. 'I will say it again, I

do hope you find this man but I don't know if I feel sorry for him. What a luxury it is to be able to desire which class you belong to. Oh, poor me, which one should I choose today: hard, back-breaking labour, or a lunch meeting in a fancy restaurant?'

'Your sarcasm is as impeccable as your cryptic crossword acumen.'

'I'll take that compliment,' she says calmly, bordering on apologetic.

I moved towards another room, and as the sweet rotting smell of the oranges faded, another familiar smell rose up. It was the smell of a body, long dead, coming from a room towards the back of the hallway.

Outside I could hear the kelpie running laps in the gravel surrounding the house, panting loudly, gasps and whimpers, like she was on edge. I should have asked help from Stevo, but I wasn't thinking clearly with the hum and static of the previous night's déjà vu continuing to ebb somewhere in the background of my skull. I crept down the hallway, to the door where the smell was strongest. It was closed but not locked.

With an unsteady hand, I opened it.

There, on a bare mattress on the floor, was the maggot ridden carcass of what looked to have once been a pig. I recoiled from the smell, the unexpected image and some unwanted flashbacks, and must have called out something because Stevo responded from outside. 'Alright?'

'Yeah,' I said, relieved that it wasn't human. I would have liked to keep looking around, but it would have to wait as if I didn't get out of there soon, I was going to throw up right in the hallway. I exited the same way I came, leaving the window as I found it. And finally did spew.

'What did you find?' Stevo said, as I came back around to the veranda.

'A few things. One: some food that has been left here in the past week. And two, a dead pig.'

Stevo was nonchalant. 'A pig? Feral, I'm guessing. What colour was it?'

'I don't know, dead colour, black, grey. I didn't hang around too long to see.'

'Happens more often than you think. Not in houses mind you, sheds and barns. They wander in and the door closes on them or they get stuck and eventually starve to death. They don't have hands, you see.'

'You're taking the piss.'

'You'd be surprised. Why don't you sit down and I'll grab some water from the ute.'

I took a seat on the steps that lead from the carport to the veranda, and closed my eyes, trying to ignore the pig body, the stench, and the déjà vu hum by attempting again to piece together this fragment of the timeline.

From what Stevo had told me: Richie was sent away to the city, to educate him, and then they enrolled him at the Bunbury ag school to learn how to help manage the farm. Instead, he went back to Perth, enrolled at one of the unis and didn't come back. And from what Kim had told me: when Richie's father got dementia, there was no one left to run the farm. But it was a lost cause, as if the land, like the gully in Mandurah, was poisoned or cursed or something, and by the look of it, for the last five or more years it had been long fallow.

This was the birth of his financial issues. Good money being thrown after bad. No one to blame but themselves. It's hard to say whether they were unlucky or lazy, the highest of insults for a farmer. You can have some bad luck if you want to work the land, but you can rely on it evening out eventually. Even stevens. Not many in these parts have walked off the land. But if you're lazy, if you don't make hay while the sun shines, then maybe you're not a farmer at all and deserve everything that comes to you. It was some ten years ago that Charlie handed it over, not by choice. Must have been a fight to remove him. Barnacled on, or whatever the farming equivalent is for an old seadog that won't leave the ship, rather go down with it than part ways. Just throw him in a hole, cover him in dirt and stones to keep the starved critters away. And yet, he had considered going to Kalgoorlie, when the farm was in its most dire state. Which seemed a betrayal. I say a betrayal – a word that has been used a lot lately – but that is unfair and doesn't sit right with me. Just like the 'missing', the 'betrayers' are no betrayers to themselves. The charge of betrayal is decided by those who have been betrayed, those that accuse and point the finger. And, yet, this accusation, the anger and rage at discovering lies and falsehoods and untruths, is misplaced – an internalised misdirection for their true feelings of fear and sorrow and foolishness at having suddenly recognised that we are never one thing.

Richie's father was not one thing, just as Richie is not one thing. No, to his family Richie is at least two things: missing and a betrayer.

'I think I might take my break now, because of the pig thing, but also because I have an important choice to make: mini-muffin or shortbread to go with my coffee,' Petal says. 'Do you need anything?'

'I'm fine,' I say.

As she walks out of the room, she hands the baton to Marcus who may have been waiting just outside the door.

She thinks she is out of earshot, but I can hear her very clearly, 'Keep him talking.'

'So where were we?' Marcus asks as he strolls in and takes the seat kept warm by Petal.

'What was the last thing you heard?'

'Something about a guy that's gone missing.'

'Maybe I should give you the summary: Richie – the guy who has gone missing – has still not been found. I have several leads that I am working on which I will put in order from most likely to least.

'One: he is running from the police because of fraud.

'Two: he is hiding at the farm, possibly to start working it again.

'Three: he is trying to rekindle a high school relationship, which is where the story heads to next.

'Four: he has killed himself.

'Five: he has murdered someone and is on the run.

'Six: he has been abducted for ransom.

'Seven: he has been murdered.

'Eight...'

'Eight?'

'Eight: he exists only in the minds of others as pure nostalgia.'

'Alright then, it is clear that you have had a little too much of the good stuff, so let's look at how we might manage that, shall we.'

I don't fight him, or try to explain myself. I feel weak and tired, so, instead, allow myself to drift into a welcoming sleep. When I wake, Marcus and Petal have again made a switch.

'You're at the farm. What happens next?' she says, with kind enthusiasm. 'The muffin was delish by the way.'

By the time we pulled the gate of the farm closed and were back on the road, it was near three in the afternoon. We went back through town, stopped in at the butchers and the bakers to grab some sausages and bread, respectively, and then at the liquor store for a block of beer, before exiting out the other end of town to head to the campsite.

Stevo was quiet, which for me felt an awkward silence. I wanted to ask more about the farm, the pig, the rotting food but thought it could wait. 'I heard Sarah say you had some kids together.'

'Three, if you can believe it. Two boys and a girl. She's the youngest. Seven this year. The boys are ten and 23. All living with Sarah now. Not the oldest. He's overseas, travelling.'

'That's a shame.'

'Yeah. Nah, they're better off. I like having them every other weekend, but not cut out for the full-time gig. You look after yours, is that right?'

'Yeah. It's good.'

'Well, good on ya.' There was sincerity in the words, but it was also clear that he was hardly envious, unflinching, maybe, in the face of modern parenting.

'So where exactly are you taking me, kidnapped as I might be?' I asked, feeling like something needed to be said.

'We are heading to this spot near the river, the Blackwood. There's an old oval, with a cricket pitch in the centre. We used to go there, groups of us, to camp and drink piss.'

'And where Richie almost drowned.'

'That's right.'

'Well colour me intrigued.'

We turned off the winding bitumen onto a dirt gravel road, near five PM. Ten minutes of driving through dusty bush until it opened on a cleared area about the size of a smaller school oval, which was less a mowed track for athletics carnivals and more a vague expanse of knee-high weeds and dry grass, sprouting through hard gravelled dirt, reds and pinks underfoot, and white wheat above. It wasn't cricket season but twenty seasons could have come and gone without a single ball being bowled given the state of it. In front, was a line of trees where the river ran. And to the left, there was a structure of sorts, a club house, the size of a small hall, on stilts, and panelled in corrugated iron, with whole sheets of wall missing such that you could see right through it in parts.

Like the farm house, it was Australian Gothic incarnate. 'Just the two of us, eh?' I asked.

'Don't worry, I won't go all Brokeback Mountain on ya! Got one of our other school mates meeting us here. He will tell you the story. It was him who pulled Richie out of the river.'

Stevo and the kelpie got out of the ute, the dog again darting away, whilst Stevo set about finding twigs and branches to start a fire. The sun was dipping, hiding itself behind the gums that skirted the west of the oval. On cue I began to feel the chill moist air, the kind that bites quickly with the coast so far away. Stevo returned with an armful of dry wood and went about assembling the tepee frame of the soon-to-be fire before grabbing a fuel can from the back of the ute, and soaking the construction in kerosene. From his pocket he pulled out his Zippo, struck the flint, and across the fumed air, sparked it into existence, the vapour whooshing excitedly, throwing sudden welcome heat.

'How about you find some more big stuff to chuck on it. There's a front coming through tomorrow, going to bring a bit of rain and will also be bringing a mighty chill right behind it. Take this beer with you,' Stevo said, as he threw an Export at me, which I caught with a fumble. He waited for me to open it, anticipating an explosion, but was disappointed with a froth fit for a beer commercial.

It was dark by the time I found what I hoped was enough wood for the night and was stacking it by the fire when another vehicle came down the way, announcing itself with the drone of a diesel engine and its blazing highbeams, spotties, and a rooftop light bar that shamed the moon by sending its shadows fleeing. When he saw the fire and Stevo's ute, he dimmed the lights courteously and slowed his own ute to a crawl to keep the dust down. The dog had run up to the vehicle, dodging and gambolling in and out of the front of it, playing a daredevil's game. A lean man jumped out and slammed the door of the old Landcruiser, already lighting a cigarette, cradling the flame of his lighter to the long cigarette before he reached us, dragging deep to make sure it stayed lit.

'You must be the doctor,' he said, blue smoke pouring from nose and mouth, lit up by the white beam of his head torch.

'I am, but John will do. Good to meet you. Mark, isn't it?'

'Yep, he said as if it were obvious, looked me over, dragged at the cigarette again, and decided he should shake my hand, squeezing it hard. He would have heard from Stevo that I was from the city, once part of the Law, and the not-a-real-doctor part he already knew, but looked to Stevo for confirmation that I was okay, can be trusted. Stevo did and Mark threw me a grin that made me feel as if we'd known each other since primary school.

'I will get me-self set up and then we will tie one on, shall we fellas?'

I set about unrolling my own borrowed swag which was caked with years of dust embedded in the canvas exterior, and when I unzipped the fly, there was a musty smell that told me it wasn't used much, and when it was it was quickly stowed away and forgotten about. Unlike the stocking of oranges, the swag smelt like an old bag of forgotten carrots decomposing at the back of a fridge's crisper. I let the swag breathe which is when I realised I hadn't brought any linen or even a sleeping bag or pillow. Stevo hadn't volunteered anything of the kind and I dared not ask for fear of pointing out that he'd forgotten, or that it was never his problem to begin with. I had a towel which would do for a blanket, and trousers and a jacket for a pillow, making do, just like it was any other stakeout of which I was far more familiar.

Unpacked, sausages sizzling away on a pan set up above the campfire, we settled in with a fresh can and our camp chairs (which Stevo had remembered) around the fire. As we waited for our dinner, Stevo told the story of the campsite. 'This was the last big fling before Richie headed to the city. The end of high school. We had about twenty of us, all set up around the cricket pitch. Had a huge bonfire going, and enough booze to destroy our livers two or three times over.

'There were our mates and some of our girlfriends and some other random girls we knew from nearby that we'd invited. We had the music going but once that was turned off at around two in the morning all you could hear was the angelic sounds of spewing and shagging.

'I think that was the night when I got Sarah pregnant. Didn't have any frangers of course. Stupid fucking kid. Me, not the one that resulted.'

Mark let out a hoot, 'You sure fucking were a stupid kid.'

'We were all pretty happy, running high after Richie almost carked it. We'll eat these snaggers and then I will show you where it happened.'

Somehow it had grown even darker by the time we'd finished eating and allowed ourselves some repose for digestion before heading to the river. And it was a dark night, with the moon barely a sliver, a nail pared from a baby's finger. You could hear the river as we approached, running quickly with the recent rains, but with our headtorches on, it looked low with thin trees barely clinging to the banks, their naked roots uncovered as if only dipping their many feet in the cold water, uncommitted to the swim. Snags created little whirlpools by the torchlight, and the red beady eyes of marron, deep in the silt below, gave away their hiding places.

'Right there is where it happened.' Stevo pointed with his head-torch to an ominous swirling vortex near the bank. 'You tell it, Mark. You saw it.'

'Anyways, so Richie was taking a piss and he was so pissed he just fell into the river, got caught by the run of the water, straight into a root and under he went. He didn't kick or yell for help. He just let it take him down, like he were asleep or something. Gone to bed in the water, pulled the river over him like a blanket. It was just lucky that I was down there also taking a piss and saw him go in. No one else was in earshot so I jumped in after him and with a bit of a fight got him to the bank. I thought he was gone, just looked dead already. I slapped him on the back which is about the best I knew in how to revive him and he kind of just burst, water pouring out of him, brown water with all mud mixed up with crushed up leaves, and bugs. And beer and tequila too for that matter.

'Before he even opened his eyes, he smiled this stupid smile and said "Ferris Bueller, you're my hero" and asked me if I had seen his beer, because the river water tasted a bit funny. Fuck me, I said, and we just had to laugh. He earned himself some sympathy from the whole incident and finally managed to hook up with Debbie for the first time. Hell of a way to make an impression.'

'The Debbie you were asking about last night,' said Stevo who had been listening to the story, nodding affirmatively to its accuracy, giggling where appropriate.

'When was the last time you saw Debbie?' I asked.

The two men conferred. 'I think she was at the school reunion. The tenth anniversary, 2005. Jesus Christ. School surely wasn't that long ago,' said Stevo, and both took long incredulous swigs of their cans and paused, contemplating the whys and wherefores of the past.

'That reunion was brutal,' Stevo said, looking at Mark for confirmation. 'It was like some horrible fucking soap opera. It was at the pub, same as where we were last night. Everyone got drunk real quick. Every conversation started with who had kids and where they were working. We found out who was gay, who was in jail, who was dead. And then it got drunker and we started talking about school, the parties, the piss-ups, car crashes, the shit we gave our teachers. Then the accusations began. About bullying and other shit. Two blokes almost had a fight. Keify and Stretch. The publican kicked them out and that was the last I heard from them. There were tears and other carry on too. One girl, Cherie, kept running up to everyone with her sleeve pulled up to show us the scars from where she had been cutting herself in high school. Wasn't necessarily a popular habit back then but she took to it. She kept telling everyone: "Look at my arm, look at what you made me do to myself."'

Mark had been waiting to jump in. 'Yeah, and you rolled up your sleeve and said to her, "Good for you, look what I did to myself when we were kids," and pointed to the "smiley" on your arm, you know, the scar you get from heating up the head of a lighter and pressing it on your skin. Looks like a smile, sort of.'

'She didn't think that was too funny and took off,' Stevo added. 'By the end of the night, it was a bit of a love in, apologies, and we could all move on.'

'And Debbie was there?' I asked, circling back.

'I'm pretty sure she was. Might have to dig us some pics to be sure.'

'And what was her last name? I might need to look her up.'

'Gibson,' Stevo said, stifling a grin.

'Gibson? Debbie Gibson?'

'Nah, just shitting ya. Debbie Turner.'

'Contact details?'

'Wouldn't have a clue.'

'Facebook?'

'Maybe, but haven't been checking in. All I know is that she doesn't live in Manji or Pembi or at least I haven't bumped into her outside of the reunion.'

'If she was even there,' Mark added with a shrug of the shoulders.

'Okay. That's going to make it difficult. What do you remember of her?'

'She was cool, a bit too clever for her own good. Gorgeous though. He was pretty lucky getting with her. But a bit boring too, if I'm honest. Although there was this one time – you remember this, Mark? – when she just let loose on our English teacher. We were studying something from Shakespeare I think, the one with the girl who is a real smart arse all the time. We'd been teasing the girls saying that she should maybe be a little less mouthy if she wanted to find a bloke. Just teasing you know. And then Debbie just let us have it, about not needing a bloke, and even if she did want one, she wouldn't pick any that came from around here. We laughed at that, called her a lezzo, and she called us in-breds. Like she wasn't a farmer's daughter herself.'

'Jeezus that was a good laugh,' Mark said, as he cracked a fresh can. 'Not the lezzo bit, but the rest of it.'

'Yep, then she told the English teacher – a woman, mind you – that she should stand up for the girls in this class instead of letting the boys run riot.'

'Yeah, and then she stormed out, slammed the door,' Mark added, and took another swig as kudos for his contribution.

'We only had one English class so she couldn't be handballed to a different one. She had to come and apologise to the teacher, right in front of us. We took pity on her and left her alone from then on. But Richie, boy, he was cuntstruck. Didn't do anything about it though. That prick could be a billionaire in a brothel and still walk out holding his own dry dick.'

'But getting drowned helped him out,' Mark added, between gulps.

'Sure did.'

The two men had taken to excited reminiscence as we returned to the camp. I followed a few steps behind, shuffling pieces around. Debbie, Richie, the letter, Jeff Buckley, the almost drowning. Jeff Buckley who did drown about three years later. They say it wasn't a suicide, just an unfortunate accident. They seemed to believe Richie's was about the same.

Back at the camp, we each eased ourselves into our camp chairs and another round was bought from the car fridge. There was a long silence, the orange glow of the fire on their faces flickered, staring into the coals, reflected in the blacks of their eyes, before Stevo took up the conversation left at the riverbank. 'It was good of Richie to let me be his best man, given that Mark saved his life and all. Either way, inviting us to the wedding, up in the city, was like him saying thanks for being my mate all those years, our history and that, but we probably won't meet again. That's how I understood it anyway.'

The fire cracked and popped noisily, demanding our attention, reminding us that tonight would be cold and that we were each alone in the cold. Stevo seemed to be comfortable with it; Mark, who I learned was still married with two kids of his own, maybe less so. I was a bit lost too, having only myself to worry about and the usual routine was out the window. No wrangling Maynard into the shower, drying the spots on his back that he misses, helping him with his pyjamas, his fragile cuddle as he goes to bed. I missed Quinn, leaning over to kiss me goodnight, her warm breasts on my chest, and me holding her arm around my waist for that bit longer, to remind me that the world will be alright if I just let it be, hearing and feeling her breath slow to a dreaming rhythm.

But I felt relaxed too and was also enjoying the male company, speaking freely, being spoken to freely. I might not have been their type but they knew how to draw me in and join them in the banter and by the end of the night I would come to understand when and where sarcasm was employed, when to speak and when to stay quiet. This is something learned and forgotten and must be relearned, so as not to overcompensate, as I was prone to do. Most of my detective life was spent with male cops, male criminals. But since the birth of Maynard the circles I ran with was a mother's group and playgroup. Just me and eight women. I was treated equally which is to say I wasn't placated as if I had everything to learn and nothing to offer. Sitting and chatting with women who were comfortable enough to breastfeed uncovered, their breasts for the time being purely functional and no longer sexual, which may have also meant that I too was not sexual. I learned to listen and allowed what could only be described as a surrogated maternal instinct to grow within me. We spoke of our struggles and celebrated quietly our children's advances and casually dismissed the setbacks by saying that they all grow and mature at different rates. It is as true for children as it is for adults in their comprehension of the aging process and manner of dealing with it.

Again, the fire cracked and flared, disturbing the silence and the interiority of our minds as if to warn us against getting too deep within our own thoughts. Stevo took the hint: 'Well, time to hit the hay,' and Mark and I understood that he was speaking for us all.

The biting cold kept me awake most of the night, seeping up from the ground and from above, and the swag did little to muffle the symphony of drunken snores. Eventually they quietened, and the babbling of the river rose, the vortexes, soothing too, beckoning to come sleep in the river and, as Mark said, pull a watery blanket over yourself, let your dreams be the stuff of the river and fish and the dark silt below.

I didn't sleep or dream straight away. Instead, the talk of reunions had got me thinking of my own 10-year reunion which, except for the self-harm, had been much the same. The dirty laundry was aired and we all got very drunk. I remember the 20-year reunion more clearly not only because it was more recent but because it was far more sober. The numbers had grown smaller, some probably thinking that the last reunion was enough. If at the 10-year we were envious and proud of our younger ourselves, bragging about what we had gotten away with, then at the 20-year we were a little embarrassed, as is the case with any revisionist-type history. We had matured, moved on, not only from the things we had done but how we remembered the things we had done. Instead, we talked of workloads, and children, and aching bodies with no sleep, and putting on weight. We laughed about it, or shook our heads in a show of dismayed solidarity. But it was also maybe a common veneer that glossed over the boredom and fear of entering our late thirties.

It was the way it had been organised – through a Facebook group – that also brought me in to contact with another high-school friend, Adam, who I hadn't spoken to for years. We friended each other, and through his posts, I saw that he was friends with Tim, another of my closest friends from primary school. Tim and I lived on the same street and spent most days after school together. He was my real-life Tyler Durden from Chuck Palahniuk's *Fight Club*: good looking, blonde-haired, blue eyed, funny, confident, academically clever and street-wise, a strong soccer and basketball player. He was an everyman, a renaissance man, and yet unique, a trendsetter, with his Skyway BMX with the white tuffs, Amiga computer, and his fashion choice of tucking his socks over the bottoms of his trackpants. He was also the first in our grade to get a girlfriend or whatever the year-seven version of a girlfriend was. It didn't appear to affect our relationship all that much – we hung out just as much as we ever had over the few months they were together. But something had changed, and everyone in our grade seemed to know about it except me. This was quite possibly the initial mental plunge into puberty, a moment in which the children, who were still children, were playing at being adults, like those they had seen on TV and in movies, with a vague idea of romantic relationships and the semblance of a commitment to each other – a precursor to what the older kids on the swings were going through. Either way, we were running at different speeds.

And another change was to come when, at the end of year seven, I learned that he was moving away, to the other side of the river. I was heartbroken. He left with no forwarding address or home phone number, and not even a proper goodbye.

It was twenty-five years later, when I friended Adam for the reunion, that I discovered that he was Facebook friends with Tim, tagging him in a post which was about terrible haircuts from the '90s, specifically the undercut – long, shoulder-length hair, clipped underneath in the style of Jason Newstead from Metallica, Mike Patton from Faith No More and even Phil Anselmo from Pantera before he opted for the skinhead look. Both Adam and I had an undercut in our mid-teens, but Tim bucked the trend with a more preppy Zac Morris from *Saved by the Bell* cut. I stalked their posts and found evidence that Tim and Adam had remained close all these years: photos of their kids playing, attending each other's' weddings. I was jealous.

I buried it, the jealousy, and made some comment on the recent post about how Tim always had the best hair, which was a poor attempt at sarcasm because it wasn't necessarily true, was a lame comment, and didn't translate well in the medium. He replied, some eight hours later with a 'thumbs up' emoticon. That hurt. Once again, and by no fault of his, at 37-years old, I felt a new kind of heartbreak, attempting to pick up our relationship from when we were best friends in year seven. But he hadn't understood it like that; instead, he responded in a way that anyone would to a vague acquaintance that was lurking over his posts. He wasn't to know that I'd been thinking about him for years, and that, when I made contact, it was my way of an apology and an attempt to recover at least some fragment of the relationship. Pathetically, I'd even hoped that he would ask me how I'd been, maybe even suggest that we might catch up if I were to ever come over to the eastern states, which is where he lived now. But he didn't as we had very different understandings of the roles each had played in the other's life. It is a cruel thing to be near middle-age and still be reminded of your naivete.

All of this, this kind of thinking, as I laid shivering in my swag, reminded me of how easy it was to fall back into memories of the past. Little encroaches and entreaties that distract and drag us away from the present. I'm not that kind of doctor, but this too is the sickness.

Petal appears to be losing interest. I can tell she is still listening, by the way she is nodding, shaking her head as if to say you poor thing. But they are too frequent, or come too late, not at the right time. Her reactions are delayed which means I have lost my audience. But who can blame her. Our pasts are our own and hardly provide the perpetuation that a good fictional story must have at its core. Even dreams, truly bizarre and fascinating imaginary experiences, lose their mystique in the hands of an ill-equipped storyteller. Which is to say that a dream is never dull, but we can make a mess of it. But I push on, fictionalising my reality in the

hope that my story will again conjure desire from my audience of one,
sometimes two.

Back to the oval.

Two days until his birthday

Despite the cold, and the thin-skinned regrets of my past, I must
have eventually fallen asleep as I was woken by warbling magpies,
laughing kookaburras and a stirring from Stevo's swag, followed by
a fart, a groan, and the tear of the long zip. I reluctantly opened
mine, because of the icy air outside. Stevo hid behind the ute to piss
before he picked up the jerry can and poured kero on the last smoking coals which exploded, bringing the small fire to life again.

I took an overdue piss myself before settling by the waning fire.

Mark was up and setting up the billy, dodging and weaving like
a boxer to keep the smoke from his eyes. 'You heading back today?'
he asked.

'Yep, hopefully I can chase up some of these leads you fellas have
given me.'

'You reckon you'll find him?'

'I'm hoping. For his family's sake.'

'You do that. Family is all most of us have got.'

Stevo dropped me back at my car in Manjimup and said goodbye, clearly with a weight on his brow. It had been a sombre
drive back, the tried-and-true conversation starters having been
exhausted; or maybe revisiting the old campground had stirred up
still waters. Sarah, the kids, Richie, Mark, old times, good times,
the farm, the dog, the ute, the bailer – all of these entwined bits
of the past and present spinning around like a chook-raffle wheel,

with the outcome of how he felt about it just as uncertain. Just like Richie I reckon. Just like myself really. This was the weight we carried, teens of the nineties, now turning 40, tallying it all up, seeing if we'd come out on top.

Despite this onset of melancholy, a mild hangover and the general feeling of ominousness that shrouded me, I returned to the motel attempting to feel upbeat, positive, as clear-headed as would allow, thinking that Debbie Turner was a very strong lead. Surely Richie almost drowning, cheating death, was a significant event in his life as well as hers, and the likely catalyst for starting up a relationship of sorts. She could be the girl he had gone to find, to rekindle their common past, recapture the raw essence of new, young love, a love that he might see as impossible with Kim and her undeniable middle-aged, middle-class presence.

I contacted Smith again, see what he could dig up for me. He gave me the brief later that day: Debbie Bowen *nee* Turner. Married to Henry Bowen. Three children, living in Albany, Western Australia. Two speeding fines in the last year. One VRO against Bowen. A series of VRO breaches by Bowen.

Some more digging, and a call to my tech guy, and I found her on Facebook. She went by the name of Debbie Olympia which immediately rang a bell: it was a town in Washington state, south west of Seattle and, even more coincidentally, was where Courtney Love – lead singer of Hole, Kurt Cobain's widow and mother to his child, Frances Bean – went to school; she even wrote a song about it on *Live Through This*. If I were to make an obvious connection, I would say I now had *two* people living in their shared past, and were quite possibly trying to find their way on a shared path, one that had diverged for some 20 years but was now coming back together.

It was then that I decided not to head back up to the city, and instead stay in Manjimup and close to Albany.

Quinn was understanding when I called.

'Maynard misses you, but he is coping just fine,' Quinn said on the phone.

'I miss you both.'

'I will take a few days off any way. I deserve it.'

'Yes, you do.'

'Call or Skype us when you can.'

I had Debbie's phone number too and sent her a purposefully dramatized entreaty. 'Hi Debbie, I am afraid that an old school friend that you might know has gone missing. His name is Richie Curtz and we are asking his old school friends for information. If you can call me or text me, that would be much appreciated. Kind regards, PD ---.'

Four hours went by with no response, and my calls went straight to voicemail. She had good reasons to screen my calls. Mistrust would be the obvious one – a random, unverified message is always something to be wary of. But she might also be avoiding contact from her husband, despite the VRO. But she might also know something: she might know Richie's whereabouts and she was scrambling to figure out the ramifications and legal implications of knowing too much, whether she will be in trouble by the law, or Richie's family.

A final option was that she didn't remember him much at all; had moved on from her high-school years, and had no inclination whatsoever to dredge up the past. Just like my primary-school friend Tim, there are people from our past that come to mind almost daily, in dreams, memories, anecdotes; their presence is almost perennially within the forefront of our thoughts even when we haven't seen them in years. Those people don't know this – that they are remembered so fondly and enthusiastically. And we can't be sure that we are in other people's thoughts either, let alone in the way we might want them to remember us. And it might just be that we are not as important or interesting as we think we are. For Debbie, Richie might not be worth remembering except as an unfamiliar face with a familiar name attached. But I don't think Richie had escaped Debbie's mind, just as I didn't think she had ever escaped his.

One day until his birthday: Albany; Meeting Debbie

Early the next day, after no response, I resent the same message. This time she responded immediately as if she had been waiting for some final sign to act.

She called instead of texting. 'Yes, I remember Richie but I haven't seen him. I am in Albany so it might be best to talk on the phone. But I am busy anyway right now, so maybe we can arrange another time. Tomorrow or the day after would be better for a call.'

'I was actually thinking of coming down from Perth, tomorrow. I could meet you.'

'His birthday is tomorrow,' she said as if puzzled that I would plan anything for the day.

'Yes, I know. Forty years old.'

'I don't think that's a good idea, coming down.'

'What about the day after?'

Debbie thought about it. 'Yeah, sure,' she said, and with the tiniest hint of excitement added, 'I can get some things together.' If she was harbouring Richie or planning some kind of elopement then she may have been buying some time to get out of there.

What she didn't know was that I had left for Albany early that morning (listening to *Live Through This*) and planned to pay her a visit at the coffee shop where she worked within the hour of the phone call, right after her lunch break.

'Ooh, that is very sneaky of you, and I like it. I also love the idea of the long-lost romance, but I don't think I could justify in my head him leaving Kim and the children. Everyone has those thoughts. Every now and then, I think about a boy I had a crush on in high school. Travis. He was gorgeous, caring, handsome. I later found out that he was gay. Absolutely clueless I was. Made it a little easier to move on, I can tell you.

'Anyway, we are so close to right now, so keep going, please.'

I arrived in Albany and almost on cue there began a light rain, misting, a long grey cloud hanging around Mt Clarence, with the town at its feet: houses built on slopes with massive granite boulders as garden features. The temperature was five degrees lower than Manjimup. When the sun did appear, it was the yellow of an old deep-tissue bruise.

It was around 2pm when I parked outside the coffee shop. It was small, quaint, with seating for around 15 people. Debbie was behind the counter, easily recognisable, with the same dark red hair, the same librarian glasses, having gone out of fashion and returned. She had added some weight, like all of us. It wasn't easy for me to hide within the limited space, and when she looked up from the counter and saw me sitting there, I could tell the jig was up. And she didn't look happy when she recognised me. I didn't expect her to.

She came to my table, but didn't make to take my order and instead took a seat across from me.

'Pleased to meet you, Debbie,' I said with a cautious smile, like an envoy meeting the leader of a military coup.

She looked at my stitches disinterestedly. 'I haven't seen Richie.'

I didn't believe her but I did my best to feign disappointment and frustration for having come this far for nothing. 'No?'

'No.'

'That is a shame. You were one of my last leads.'

'Well, sorry to burst your bubble.' She was curt, anxious.

'I understand that you might be worried that our contact could cause a stir with your ex-husband. Would there be a better place for us to talk?'

She didn't like that. 'I gave you a better time, but you chose to ignore it. Anyway, we are back together now. And he is working on his trust issues so this could be a good test for him.' She looked around as if checking that Henry hadn't wandered in without her notice. 'How long has Richie been missing, anyway?'

'Months now. His wife and children, two girls, are very upset.'

Debbie's eyes darted side to side, conjuring an image of them. 'I bet they are beautiful.' She began to wipe absently at the table with a dirty tea towel that otherwise sat on her shoulder leaving a damp shadow on her cream polo shirt, the name of the café handstitched on the pocket. 'He deserves to be happy. I hope he is okay.'

She was difficult to read. I had seen it before in domestic violence cases. A woman who has necessarily become practiced in keeping her emotions in check, to soothe her husband's rage, fuelled by jealously and paranoia. But she also seemed to be opening, as if the past were slow-releasing pleasure endorphins, chemically reacting, allowing for emotion – any emotion – to surface.

'We all hope he is okay,' I said sombrely as I drew the pink envelope from my pocket and handed it over to her. 'Was this letter from you?'

She didn't recognise the envelope immediately, but did seem to understand its consequence as she removed the letter, unfolded it gently, like sacred parchment, and began to read.

A smile rose on her face, but then it tightened, her jaw at the sides bulged as her teeth came together and I could see her chest rising quicker and quicker, a deep flush on her neck. And then, quite unexpectedly, she exploded joyously: 'Oh my God, yes, I wrote this letter. Isn't it silly. God, we were so in love. Or at least we thought we were. He used to sing to me, you know. Jeff Buckley songs. Nobody can sing like Jeff Buckley but the words and the truth on his face made me want to cry and laugh and hold him. He was so cute.

'He even made me a mixed tape with all his favourite love songs. "For Debbie" it said in black Artline. There were about 12 songs over the two sides. Jeff Buckley, of course. "Lover You should have come over", "Lilac Wine." But there was also Stone Temple Pilots' "Interstate Love Song" and "Still Remains", Pearl Jam's "Black", Nirvana's "About a Girl", others I can't remember now. I still have it. We had CDs back then but we couldn't load them on to the computer yet, or burn them on to a disk, or at least we didn't know how. And the only tape deck we used was the one in his old Holden ute. He had inherited the ute from his grandfather, just an old farm one. He had me in the driving seat most times while he was outside pushing it. There was rust all through it, bald tires, brakes that sort of worked, and it kept on jumping out of gear too. There was definitely no point in spending much money on a new CD player for the ute. So we just listened to the radio, or listened to the tape which was enough for us.'

She stopped, taking a breath, and dropped her gaze, embarrassed at having disclosed so much, and so uninhibited. I had been wrong about her: she hadn't seen him, the way she spoke, the excitement, the recollection of a memory, a time-capsule of emotion buried for decades, was opened right in front of me.

I waited for her to gather herself. 'Why did you break up?'

'We were never really together. He was always away in Perth for school, and when he came back we had to try and pick things up where we left off which was never really clear. It was always awkward and we weren't left alone very often just because his friends wanted to see him as well. We could never really connect beyond the first night we shared together, as if we couldn't be together as partners enjoying normal things, normal conversations, about family, pets, sport, any small talk type things where we get to know each other. He wouldn't even have known my middle name or my birth date. But I remember his. We loved each other, but it was exhausting and impractical and cannot be lived in real life. Everything had to be serious; there was no "fun" when we were together. It was just always dark, and moody, but wonderful too. And then there was some trouble at his boarding school and he spent more time getting drunk and we saw less and less of each other and then eventually he didn't call.

'Richie and I joked about moving to Seattle, or at least visiting it sometime. That was where the world was happening. And then we would move to Twin Peaks. We loved that show. Just kids talking. Wanting to get out, just like every teenager living in a dead-end town. I wouldn't have my time again, but sometimes I wonder. Albany was about as close as I got to something that resembled Twin Peaks. Now I'm just like the Shelley character from the show, working at a coffee shop with an abusive husband. And now I have a strange detective questioning me. Maybe this is Twin Peaks.'

'Not so strange, although 1990's Kyle MacLachlan's good looks and hair would be a welcome change. Do you think he wants to meet you again?'

Debbie thought on this, eyes searching the table for an answer. She was thinking about all the 'what ifs' if he did return. She was thinking of her two daughters and her son, and the upheaval they would experience, for a third time – them first moving out from the family home to a hotel, then moving back in again. She was listing in her head the life she had: their house, their cars, their insurance premiums, their school, the subjects her children were studying, the pathway to university or an apprenticeship for the boy. She was thinking of their superannuation, their term deposit, their mortgage. She was thinking of their new sensible friends, the parents of their children's friends. She was thinking of the meal she was going to cook that night, the shopping she needed to do beforehand, the TV shows she was going to watch tonight before falling asleep on the couch or in her sexless bed. She will need to buy cheese, and wine, and she wants to drink but should watch her weight. Richie would destroy all this if he were to come to her today, an upheaval, no matter how much he had changed and how much she needed things to be different.

But this was not what she was thinking at all. 'I would hope so. I would hope he comes to find me. And I would hope that he hasn't changed a single bit and that he would drag me away from this small coffee shop, just for an hour and remind me what being young was all about.'

As she spoke, Debbie's gaze had been fixed on some point behind my shoulder, outside of the café towards the carpark. Fixed but not focussed. But something had come into her line of vision, occupied the empty space and stolen her attention. Her words began to falter, as if confused, and she paled. My back was to the entrance so I turned to see where she was looking. Outside, at the window, there looked to be a young man, in his late teens or early twenties, his hands cupped around his eyes so as to better see inside. But he was hard to see because the sun had now revealed itself and was reflecting off of wet roads and cars, the outside looking more like a photo negative. I turned back to Debbie, and saw a slight movement of her brow, an intensity in her eye, and she made the slightest shake of her head, as if warding him off, like a spirit that was too early to take her. I looked around again and saw his profile as he walked away quickly: a weak chin and auburn hair.

'So, they had a boy together. That's what his father was saying. His father knew all along. Does Richie know? You will have to tell me. Did he leave because of the boy, did he go looking for the boy, or has he disappeared because of the boy. Maybe he left in shame. Does he want the boy to find him? Is that what this is all about?'

'Patience,' I say intolerably. 'Patience.'

'It's been running out you know. It's lucky I am stuck here as much as you are.'

'I better get back to it,' Debbie said, getting up too quickly from the table, upsetting the salt and pepper shakers. 'The spoiled little shits from school will be coming in soon and they'll be wanting their milkshakes.'

'Who was that at the window, if you don't mind me asking?'

'That is . . . my eldest son.' She was staring at the same spot on the table, and began polishing it again with concerted effort, trying her darndest to look as if he were of little importance. 'There's not much more I can tell you. About Richie. That is all in the past. But I hope you do find him.'

'You have my number.' As I got up from the table, and made my way to the exit, I also tried my darndest to look calm and above all uninterested in the stranger at the window. And I knew that, as soon as I was out the door, Debbie would be contacting the boy to give him some warning.

Outside, I scouted the street but was hampered by my eyes still adjusting to the wet glare. That was until the bark of an exhaust coming from a burgundy single-cab HiLux caught my attention. It was leaving the car park but I could just make out an old P-plate stuck to the tailgate and a head of red hair behind the steering wheel. I wasn't in the mood for a car chase so I memorised the rego and went back to the hotel, looked him up and began figuring out how I was going to deal with this new information. As far as I knew, Debbie only had the three children, all to her current husband. But this boy was also her son and the uncanny resemblance to Richie suggested that he was Richie's son, likely conceived in their early twenties and only a few years older than Richie and Kim's eldest daughter. Petal had raised some good questions [*Thank you*]. Did Richie know about him? Did the son know about Richie? Smith's theory about a secret family suddenly seemed a lot more plausible. But Debbie's reaction to the letter didn't seem to fit this scenario. Did Richie find out about the son and has come to make amends? The river of meaning must widen before it narrows.

I made some calls that night. Debbie did have another child. Frank, Francis, Francis Bean. Born October 15, 1997, five-foot-eleven. There was no registration of the father. She might not have seen Richie recently but that didn't mean she hadn't told him about the boy in the past twenty or so years since. And if not – if she hadn't told him about Frank – had he learned it himself?

I was ready for bed but was also desperate to Skype home before it got too late.

'Daddy, my tooth is coming through, see,' Maynard said as he pulled Quinn's phone up close to his mouth so I could see. There amongst the pink desolation was an undeniable ridge of bone white.

Zero days until his birthday: Albany; Bluff Knoll

I woke up in my motel room on Albany highway, having slept an exhausting sleep, my head throbbing and scrambled, the laughter circling like squawking birds, waiting to see the past, just beyond my periphery, even with my eyes closed.

I could hear traffic, larger vehicles, but no rain.

It was the morning of Richie's fortieth birthday. And the only fact I could be certain of was that he wasn't found. I hadn't found Richie for his birthday. He should be waking up in his home, with his wife, with his kids, being celebrated, hard to buy a present for so they get him a Bunnings voucher, cooked breakfast, eggs how he likes them.

If I were optimistic, I could argue that it was still early in the day, and his birthday was not over yet. And it was only Tuesday and his party is on the weekend. Plenty of time to get him home, scrubbed up, costume washed, come as you were. And I was certain that I was closer than I had ever been. Still, it felt as though the moment had passed.

It was too early to ring Kim to see how she was going. Or it wasn't too early at all; it's just that I didn't want to have to make the call and state the obvious. This was nothing like the calls I had made as a cop, in both nature and delivery; the kind I made to a family to tell them that their teen daughter has been killed in a car crash, or their son has been stabbed outside a Northbridge nightclub. With a partner, we would go to the parent's home, ask to come inside. The details were unequivocal: pronounced dead at 1.35 AM, knife wound to the chest, through the heart, DOA, body to be collected from . . . . This would be translated into: 'I have some unfortunate news to tell you, can we sit down?' We would sit and without delay or euphemism state: 'Your son was stabbed in Northbridge and was killed.' There is shock, disbelief, anger, and eventually, over time, a sense of closure from which healing could begin. This was the solace I couldn't offer Kim: all I could tell her was that the tragedy that she was undergoing in her life would necessarily continue beyond the arbitrary date by which we hoped he would be found.

So, I made a coffee with the motel sachets and finished off the half-eaten croissant from yesterday's breakfast. I hadn't been hungry, not since Manjimup, my guts still not feeling right, and there was always the nausea. I considered another coffee before calling Kim but that would be delaying the inevitable and, instead, I ripped it off like a Band-Aid. I thought she wouldn't pick up, but she did. She was in tears. The kids were still prepping for school which was a good enough excuse for her to tell me she didn't have time to talk.

'I know you have tried,' she said, with veiled disappointment.

'He is out there. Ready to come home,' I replied. Vacuous words, clutching at straws, and hard to tell if I believed them myself.

'It doesn't matter now. If he is alive and well, then he mustn't want to be here. He doesn't want to come home. And if he did make it home, then I'm not sure we can forgive him anyway. If he is dead . . . if he is dead, that we can forgive.'

She hung up. There was no mention of meeting again or, indeed, of the substantial fee that had accrued. It wasn't the time to talk money and I felt guilty for even thinking of it. But by the end of the day, there was a correct sum of money in my account, plus about 10 percent above my estimate. As far as Kim was concerned, all was settled.

All this time, since taking the case, I hadn't told Kim about the déjà vu I'd been experiencing, feeling that it would only offer some vague, irrational hope. And, yet, even as I was speaking to her over the phone, and whilst packing the car to make the long trip home, I could still hear faint laughter, and the feeling of being stalked by familiarity. And an even stronger feeling that I was being watched.

This was in part the paranoia that followed the episodes, but it turned out that I was actually being watched. Richie's son's – Frank's – very conspicuous Hilux was parked a little down the street. He was staking me out, not very well, unfortunately. I felt again for the stitches above my eye. Had he been on my tail this whole time?

I didn't make a show of recognising him, and continued to pack in no real hurry. Only when I started the car did he make a move, making a U-turn and driving away from me. Which is when I decided to do a bit of tailing myself. He knew my car and I knew his so there was no point in keeping too much distance between us. I stayed at about five car lengths away, front and centre in his rear-view mirror. He didn't try to lose me, we just drove, out of Albany, heading where I was heading, north up the highway, doing the speed limit. It was near Mount Barker, almost an hour into the drive, when he put his right indicator on. A sign had 'The Porongurups' written on it, indicating the Porongurup range, standing out over the plains to the east, rising out of nothingness, like alien constructions that had no place here. [*Petal, a local of the area, is smiling proudly, as if she were in fact the alien that put them there*].

If it wasn't clear that I was officially tailing him before, then following him at the turn gave it away. Which is likely why he sped up to 130 kays – 20 over the limit. I tried to keep pace but he overtook some grey nomads in their four-wheel drive towing a caravan, him swerving across a double line, the sound of a blaring horn from a car coming the other way which he nearly collected. I was stuck behind the caravan with no safe opportunity to pass for near 15 minutes. Only when we came to a T-junction was I just able to see him turn left – right would have taken him back to Albany. We were heading north-east, far from my intended destination. We weaved our way through the range for another 30 kilometres, with Frank mostly out of sight. I thought that I had lost him, except that at the red-dirt turnoff for Bluff Knoll there was a drift of dust indicating that a vehicle had gone that way. I followed it (neglecting to pay the National Park admission fee) and after another five minutes reached the carpark, where I found the lone HiLux. I parked far enough away from him to enable myself some escape room if it came to that. But the car looked empty and, as I made a quick walk over to it, I found no one and nothing except the detritus of an out-of-control fast food habit inside. I looked around the car park, checked the toilets, finding more of nothing. Beckoning was the path leading upwards towards the dark sheer face of the knoll looming above. It was the only way he could have gone and he had a 10-to-15-minute head start on me. The trees made it difficult to see the track but I was sure I saw him disappearing into the bush. I wasn't prepared for hiking, in body or equipment, but I was going to be climbing it. I threw on my sneakers, swapped my jeans for a pair of shorts, and grabbed a 500ml water bottle, three-quarters filled. It was still cool, despite the sun, and likely much cooler at the top, which allowed me to justify within myself that that amount of water was enough. A sign told me it was 1098 metres above sea level and was a 3-4-four-hour hike. If this proved to be nothing, then I would be getting home very, very late. But there was a beating in my chest that told me I had to follow the boy to the top of the hill.

The trail began with an easy concreted path, before becoming rockier with concrete steps reinforced with rebar. With each step I could hear my knees, clicking like a ratchet, a hip joint that sounded vaguely like a snapping twig, and gravel sliding under my unsteady feet. An hour of climbing later and my pulse was throbbing in my ears, and my water was empty. When had I gotten so old, so unfit, so stupid? I should have turned back, used my head, my training, but I could still feel that second pulse, something outside of my body, drawing me further up the path. A drum beating around me, the muffled jungle techno bass of a nightclub toilet. The beat increased, and I pushed myself, feeling the sweat on my back, cooled by the breeze, further and further.

Just over half way and I was sweating and swearing and making oaths to eat better, exercise more, be smarter. I also began to think about what I would say when I saw the boy. I would ask him questions, about his father, his true father, and whether he knew that he was his true father. I wondered whether he would be defensive, backed into a corner; would he lash out or would he run. Did he want to know the truth? And what was the point if the father he had never known may himself never be found?

Another hour of hard climbing, where I contemplated the names of the scrub and trees that I didn't know, pondered why cold air sinks but the temperature was dropping the higher I went, and wondered how long it must have taken to cut in the steps for the hike. And then I was standing at the top, a wide expanse at the summit, flat, but with shards of rock and scrub.

Eastwards was the straight drop over the edge, hundreds of metres, with no guardrail or even a warning sign. Just you and the void.

In that moment I understood Richie's romanticism, the overwhelming beauty and awe. And if it wasn't for the blistering cold wind drawing fat goosepimples from my flesh, I might have forgotten why I was there in the first place.

I looked around, behind trees, rocks, any hiding places, finding no one. I was baffled until I saw him emerge from the trail from where I had just come. He'd hidden and waited for me to pass, followed me. I was close to the cliff edge, cornered, Frank standing no more than five metres away, dressed like he was ready for a hike, almost as if he had always planned to come to Bluff Knoll on that day, planned for this moment.

'Have you seen my father. Have you met him?' he said, calmly across the whipping breeze.

'No. I thought I would have, but no. I never imagined I would be speaking to his son instead.' As I spoke, I slowly circled around him, towards where the edge wasn't so stark, and where other paths allowed for an escape. 'What do you know about him?'

'Not much,' Frank said, matching my movement, keeping the same distance between us. 'Mum told me he was dead, ever since I was a baby. Nothing else. That's until she heard he was missing a few months ago. He knew about me. She was scared that he would come back and that Henry would find out. So, she told me the truth. She told me a bit about what he was like when she knew him, where he grew up.'

'It was you who visited the farm recently, didn't you?'

'Yeah.'

'I found the dead pig.'

'That was a gift for him if he decided to come back. Kinda cruel but I was pissed off. The prick deserved it.'

'I get it.'

'Mum told me about you last night. You're a detective. So, what do you know about him now?'

'I know a bit. You look a lot like him. I know that for sure. I have a photo in the car, if you want to see. I can tell you some more about what I know.'

He looked around, across the range. 'It's a bit late for that,' looking now at the path behind. Looking for witnesses. There was no one coming. He took a few steps towards the cliff edge.

'Don't do it,' I said, louder now.

He turned to me, confused. 'I would never. Just look,' and he turned again to the cliff edge, and gestured at the horizon.

I followed his gaze, and, as best I could, appreciated the moment, the peace; that is until a sense of unease drifted over me, and saw a shadow creeping up towards us, across the flat plain below, like a dark transparent rolling tidal wave. I looked for a cloud above but there was none, just pure cold white-blue sky. I braced myself as the wave of the shadow engulfed me and everything dimmed. I felt unsteady. I looked for Frank, but he had gotten past me, his back turned, heading away and down, a vanishing point. Alone but not alone, the laughter from the crowd, just out of sight, to my left, and a scream that had already happened. And I spun to look, determined to finally catch the vision from the past, but it wasn't possible.

And then, as much as I can remember, the world was black.

Petal has an eyebrow raised, quizzical, unsure, sceptical. 'You are saying that this is what happened to you. It wasn't a suicide attempt. That you met Richie's son and then almost saw a ghost from the past, and then became disoriented and fell?'

'That was my experience, yes.'

'Where's my notepad? I have something I need to underline.'

Strange voices: 'He is waking up. Can you hear me? Do you know where you are?'

A woman and a man, on their knees, staring down at me. The sun was high behind them making it difficult to distinguish their faces. The woman leaned in, held my eyes open to check for signs of life. 'Can you hear me? What is your name?'

'Francis?' My head hurt, ebbing and flowing between a dull throb and an ice pick to the temple.

'Don't move, Francis. We think you . . . fell.' The pair looked at each other, exchanged what looked like knowing glances, and then she pointed to a spot behind her. 'From that ledge up there.'

'I'm not Francis.'

'He's in shock,' the woman said to the man as she tucked in the sides of a jacket they had draped around me. 'We will need to get you to the hospital. You hit your head when you fell. And your leg is broken. And your arm doesn't look right.'

I looked down to my leg and saw that a clean edge of a white bone was sticking out from what was supposed to be my shin. I closed my eyes, trying to eradicate the uncomfortable image by piecing together what had happened. 'Did you see a young man? In hiking clothes? Did you see him?'

They looked at each other again, this time making no attempt to disguise their concern.

'Yes, we passed him on our way up,' said the man, factually, placatingly. 'We won't catch him now.'

'Let's sit you up a little, so that you can have some water,' said the woman.

With their help, I shuffled my body gingerly, bracing my right arm with the left, keeping my leg still. Only then did I see their daughter, sitting by herself at a distance, between the slabs of rock and scrub, barely five-years old, legs crossed, looking over her shoulder at me. She had a stick in her hand and was absently drawing spirals in the air.

'Don't look, honey,' her mother said, not for the first time. The girl looked away, back to her spirals.

'We will need to splint your leg or do something until the ambulance or helicopter gets here,' the man said.

'Thank you.'

'You might want to thank your lucky self.'

A rescue helicopter did airlift me out. I again thanked the woman and man (I forget their names) and apologised to my rescuers for what I hadn't gotten myself into.

The remainder of the day was filled with green-tinged waiting rooms and scans, histories taken of previous medical issues, and then an operation to reset the bone in my leg. The arm was only dislocated and could be massaged back into place. And the other wounds were taken care of with a few more stitches added to my ragged body. I woke up groggy from the operation but was warm and cosy and allowed myself to fall in and out of a blissful sleep, one that comforted me, numbed me, left me feeling like I didn't have a single care for anything else in the world.

When I was ready to be moved from recovery, had 'evacuated' my bowels, I was brought to a room where I slept the whole night. I woke only because of the sound of clacking heels and the dragging of a chair to my bedside – a smartly-dressed female councillor was paying me a visit. 'How are you feeling?' she asked, with a practiced kindness that was not overly empathetic but also gave little away about her real intentions.

'Okay, but a little confused.'

'Do you know what happened?'

Another lie: 'I remember blacking out and fell. That's about it.'

'The people who found you believe that you didn't fall. They said you may have jumped.'

This caught me off guard. 'No, that's not what happened,' I said adamantly, but took far too long in thinking of some feasible explanation for otherwise. 'No, I had seen someone I was looking for. I spoke to him, and I must have lost my balance.'

'Okaaay.' She didn't look or sound convinced. 'Nevertheless, we will be having someone watch you just to be sure. I'm sure you understand.'

It was then that I saw a large male nurse, Marcus, hovering at the door, and behind him, a stern and stoutish nurse with a pen and pad for once-only notetaking.

| 3 |

One day after his birthday: Albany hospital

It is at this point, this moment in time, that we have made a return to the present – the day after Richie's birthday – to me in my hospital bed, the day after surgery, the time spent telling my story to Petal. But her shift has ended, back-to-back ten hours and she needed some rest, and to be with her family. Marcus has also left for the day. I was on my own.

I still hadn't contacted Quinn yet, to tell her what had happened. She had been calling me, every other hour, and it wouldn't be long before she started to call the police stations and hospitals. As far as she was concerned, I was missing – I was missed. I'd given her a list of places – motels in Manjimup and Albany – where I might have stayed, and the days I would be there. But they would tell her that I am not there.

I said to myself that I was trying to maintain some privacy for the persons involved. This was why I hadn't contacted her. But this was not true. I hadn't told her that I was lying in a hospital bed 600 kilometres away because, for the first time in what seemed to be a very long time, I was alone. I was anonymous. I was not a husband or a father there. I was not a detective. I was not a man, near forty. I was a patient, an invalid, who was physically incapable of taking care of his responsibilities. I had a broken leg and cracked ribs. And

I was free. They thought I had gone missing, but I was far from missing.

What I was was selfish, stubborn, and blissfully drugged. I was also pre-emptively indignant at how I might be thought of when Quinn learned that I was in hospital. She would worry, fuss, like Petal. I was a man and I could handle being on my own. I gave up my mum years ago when she cut out the police recruiting ad and kicked me out. I hadn't looked back since.

But there was also a full bottle of my own cold piss sitting on the table next to me, telling me that I was not as capable or as free as I thought. And the morphine which was injected into my right buttock only 15 minutes ago was starting to take effect, and I sank deeper and deeper into the bed, into the womb.

Two days after his birthday

The following morning, still a little groggy, constipated, with pangs of hunger and guilt, I did call Quinn. And because I missed Maynard. And because I owed him. Because a parent's love is duty, responsibility, as much as it is love.

Quinn was silent on the phone. No 'hello' or 'why haven't you called' or 'where have you been' or 'I've been worried sick.' Just silence which maybe was less a show of anger and more a disguised sense of hurt – that I didn't love her enough to feel the need to call her, or that I didn't know how much she loved me.

I broke the divide with a pre-emptive 'Everything's fine,' before steering the conversation into more neutral territory. 'How's Maynard?'

'Fine.'

'Can I speak to him?'

'No.'

'Why?'

'He is at school.'

'Touché.'

'Don't do that. Don't joke. He wants to know where you are.'

There was estrangement in our voices, doing what estranged couples do, communicating our feelings through our child. I am the estranged father, the part-time custody dad who skipped his fortnightly weekend with his son to go fishing with his buddies. She is the mother at home picking up the emotional pieces of our son's shattered expectations.

'So, where are you?' The question began in frustration, having had to repeat herself, but had softened by its end.

I lied and told her I had been out of mobile range, which was still feasible in some parts of the south west. I told her that I would be a few more days. In Albany. Still finding some details. Think of those poor girls missing their father, I said. I didn't feel good about myself.

A pause. 'Come home soon,' she said, a tender imploration, ever the peacemaker.

'I will,' and her side of the line died before I could tell her I love her.

Thankfully, before I could deconstruct the call, a suited man with an affable demeanour was standing in the doorway. If I were to settle on a face, I would say the jowly Mister Drummond *from Diff'rent Strokes*. Petal, whose shift had started, stood immediately behind him, seemingly intrigued more than duty-bound. They came in, waiting to be invited, like kindly vampires. He stood at the foot of my bed, whilst Petal took her usual seat.

'Hello, John?'

'Yes, that's right.'

'Nice to meet you. I am Doctor Hilton. Greg Hilton. I'm the neurologist here and have some information about your test results.'

He looked professionally neutral which I chose to ignore with good humour. 'Fantastic. Anything unusual?'

'The word is that you either jumped or maybe fell off of that rise at the Bluff. I think I can clear up the dispute.'

'I didn't jump,' I said, imploringly. 'I didn't,' and looked to Petal for confirmation.

Hilton looked to Petal also. She nodded her head slowly, her eyes closed, her ritual of agreement.

'No, I agree,' he said, almost upbeat, confident in Petal's assessment of my character, but more so by the data he had on his clipboard. 'The witnesses said it looked as if you threw yourself over the edge which is why they thought you had attempted to take your life. But, in their statements, they also said that you were shaking violently before you fell, and taking this into consideration, and after having looked at the scans for your concussion, I believe you in fact had an epileptic seizure – Tonic Clonic to be exact, or what used to be called a Grand Mal. This likely caused you to black out, lose your balance and fall. This is also to say that you may have late onset epilepsy. Do you have any family history?'

I felt blind-sided, even when I shouldn't have: my maternal grandmother had severe epilepsy and migraines, and lived a mostly-cloistered life because of it. Which is also why I had only ever witnessed her seize once, when I was young, nine-years old, maybe, my mother, sister, brother and I visiting her in her darkened home, curtains closed. In the kitchen, making us tea and scones, as we waited in the bunker-like living room, and then a shattering racket. The four of us racing towards the noise. A woman on the floor, shaking, broken crockery and hot black tea from a pot spilled on linoleum. I saw my grandmother, her permed grey-blonde hair, her comfortable nightgown and mothers' day slippers; but she was not my grandmother: there was only a trembling, shaking body dressed as my grandmother, and what could only be described as an absence of her being. This is the uncanny unease that horror feeds on, the threat of the strange. My mother, experienced since her childhood, cleared away the dangers, and comforted her own mother, made her safe, not as a daughter to her mother, but as a nurse attending a patient. 'It's okay, Jenny, it's okay,' my mother repeated. We ran from the room, us three kids, fleeing the possessed woman who had only moments ago been our grandmother. We turned on the television, turned it up loud, desperate to watch anything that would replace the discomfiting images that lay behind our impressionable eyes.

At the Bluff, I know only of a blackout, an absence. There are no discomfiting images for the possessed. Only for a little girl drawing spirals in air.

'We will need to get you to Perth for an MRI as soon as possible to be sure that it is what I think it is. We can release you, but unfortunately you won't be able to drive, just in case you have another episode. Not that you could anyway.' He looked at my leg and frowned.

Despite the so-called freedom I had only just now proclaimed to have found, it was time to call Quinn again and confess and ask that she come get me. I am a drunk 16-year-old, at 1 AM, with no money for a taxi home, reverse-calling from a payphone.

Three days after his birthday

Quinn left Maynard with her mother and caught a bus down with the intention of driving my car back, having been retrieved from the Bluff carpark. She didn't come immediately – she had clients that needed rescheduling and was informed by the nurses that I couldn't be discharged just yet anyway. She called when she was in Albany and again when she was at the hospital. She spoke to the attending nurses, she spoke to Petal, before coming to my room. She heard from them the disproven accusation of my suicide attempt. She looked at my leg, my pale drawn face, sat beside me, held my hand and cried.

I squeezed her hand back, soothed her, told her it's okay.

She didn't buy it. 'You should have called me earlier. You should have told me what had happened.'

'I didn't want to worry you.'

'Bullshit. That's not for you to decide.'

I could have offered a retort, but, the recent shot of morphine didn't allow for the conversation to maintain any real heat or longevity, as I steadily drifted into a pleasurable embracing sleep that knew only pacifism.

When I woke, Petal was completing some notes and talking with Quinn about my care plan.

Marcus was also there, with a wheelchair, to escort me out of the hospital and into a patient transfer service to take me to Royal Perth Hospital to redress the leg.

Quinn made the seven-hour journey home by herself. 'I will see you at RPH.' She kissed me on the forehead and it felt warm, and lingered long after she had gone.

'Time to take a little break from the detecting, don't you think,' Petal said with a wink as I was lifted into the ambulance.

'I do. Thank you for listening.'

'Find that man, but not at any cost. Because it is Maynard that you are here for, no-one else.'

The morphine wore off at Kojonup, about halfway into the trip. I wasn't to know but the last one was the last one. From then on it was Panadeine Forte, and then Panadol, all part of the weaning process.

In Perth, at the hospital, the wound was examined, redressed again. The doctor said that I could go home. They loaned me a wheelchair, but tested me on crutches, and let me take myself to the toilet which I appreciated, having spent the last three days with a piss bottle, and shitting in a pan on my bed.

Home again, and when we arrived, Maynard was sprinting out to the driveway, grinning wide, oblivious to everything I had done, and everything I had thought. He was intrigued by my cast and took care when I warned him of my sore ribs when he hugged me. It was good to be home.

An appointment was made for an MRI for a week's time, during which I laid on the couch, leg elevated as instructed to keep the swelling down. I watched TV, sitcoms, reruns, my favourite movies, binging Netflix. I played video games. I drank coffee and ate chocolate, trying to distract myself from the little throbs of pain shooting through my leg.

I'd suggested to Quinn that we keep it between ourselves until the MRI. Explaining it to my parents or hers, or my siblings, would only complicate matters. No visitors, except for Silver Chain nurses, and Smith, who, when I answered the door on my crutches, slunk past me carrying the stink of cigarettes and guilt on him. 'I shouldn't have let you go by yourself,' he said as he eased himself into a chair whilst I arranged myself on the lounge.

'I'm a big boy and can take care of myself. I wanted to.'

'So you say.' Smith rubbed his muzzle of beard, unhappy and unsatisfied. 'I heard a bit of a story about Bluff Knoll.'

'Quinn called you, didn't she?'

'She sure did. First time we'd spoken in years. She isn't happy with either of us. You almost died. Do you ever think about that?'

'It wasn't that big of a fall,' I said, dismissing it as nonsense.

'Oh, no? If you had been standing only a few metres to the left, then you would have fallen a long, long way and you wouldn't be talking to me today. Dead. Kaput. Goneski. There is no way they can put that humpty dumpty back together again.'

I couldn't help smile at that. 'Bullshit. You know I am a hard-boiled detective. I don't bust up that easily.'

We smirked at each other, both knowing this wasn't true at all: I am a gooey stay-at-home father.

'He's out there, Smithy. I met Francis, his son. I can still help.'

'Hey, forget about it. I don't have any skin in that game, but you do. So, once again, pretty please, start looking after yourself. Take it from me, you don't want to be divorced at your age, and that boy of yours shouldn't be without his dad.'

'I know.'

'Anyway, I got work to do, bad guys to catch.'

'Let me know if you hear anything,' I said, falsely noncommittal from the lounge.

Halfway out the door, Smith eyed me one last time. 'Maybe.'

I had the MRI, followed by a meeting with the specialist, a short man, humbly suited, and barely out of his twenties.

'Is this your first seizure?' he said, as if it were a very ordinary question and my falling off a cliff quite commonplace.

'Yes, nothing before this. That I am aware of.'

'Nothing out of the ordinary. Lapses in memory or feeling vague.'

My gut and my heart traded places for a moment. 'Yes, definitely yes, very out of the ordinary, memory lapses and vagueness.' I explained the moments of déjà vu, from walking home from school at 17, to Bluff Knoll one week ago, and everything in between. He wrote it all down, nodded his head as if it all made sense, and gave me the news. 'Well, the incident when you were 17 is what we call an absence seizure and the feeling of déjà vu is very common with the aura experienced during temporal lobe seizures.' He then reached into a nearby drawer and fished out a pamphlet and read out the bullet-pointed description of a temporal lobe seizure:

- *A sudden sense of unprovoked fear or joy*
- *A déjà vu experience — a feeling that what's happening has happened before*
- *A sudden or strange odour or taste*
- *A rising sensation in the abdomen, similar to being on a roller coaster.*

'It seems you have been having these mini seizures for quite a while. They aren't necessarily a problem but they are often the precursor to a Tonic Clonic which is what you have had and is something we will need to treat. I have a particular medication in mind that we can trial.'

He wrote a script and handed it to me. 'This should hopefully minimise the chance of any seizures but we will need to schedule regular check-ups to make sure we have it right. You still won't be able to drive for at least six months, I'm afraid.'

I thanked the doctor and Quinn spoke with him privately, just as she would if it were Maynard who was sick. She then drove me to the pharmacy to buy the medication that I will likely be taking for the rest of my life.

At home, over coffee, we both read the pamphlet. The gist: I need to be careful around water, heights, sharp objects, electrical equipment, irons, and hair driers; if on a bike, I need to stay away from busy roads; if I am swimming or bathing, make sure there is a lifeguard or responsible adult nearby; and never lock the door.

Quinn took it well, even though it was clear that behind the compassionate smile, she was furiously processing how she was going to handle looking after two children for a while. We joked to ease our minds:

'Well, I guess we won't be taking that snorkelling and surfing holiday in Hawaii this year,' Quinn said with a stifled laugh.

'And I won't be able to ride in the Tour de France this year.'

'We certainly shouldn't go rock climbing.'

'And I won't be able cut up things, or style my hair.'

It felt good to laugh, the first time in weeks, even if it was in the shadowed face of uncertainty.

Within days of taking the medication, the episodes, or, maybe more accurately, the symptoms I'd been experiencing most of my adult life had completely ceased: no more déjà vu; no cloud of dread hanging about me; no voices, or laughter; no fear of screaming out, or of having already done so. Though not completely gone was the new paranoia and nervousness that came from my diagnosis; the awareness that my body could, at any moment, do what it pleased, the brain and consciousness relieved of its control. And control is everything. I hear Ian Curtis of Joy Division. I see him dancing, front of stage, awkward limbs and strange angles. I imagine him being diagnosed with epilepsy. I imagine him taking his own life, hung in his kitchen, his lifeless body, still, controlled. (Petal would tell me to get those thoughts out of my head.)

This was all unquestionably good news. There are others that are worse affected and where treatment is no option. I am grateful. For myself and my family. And I should have been happy, fearless, thankful that I was normal, healthy. Except that the medication had stolen something else away: the feeling that there was more to the world than the everyday would suggest, some other realm or dimension that I was able to peer into, step into. I had, in a sense, been holding onto that possibility, wanting to believe that there was some metaphysical twist in the mortal tale, something beyond what can be observed, something transcendent. Some have the un-seen realm of Heaven, some believe in an afterlife, ghosts, spirits. I had believed that there was a past that was trying to return to our present, or that there was a present that wanted to connect to the past. Now, there was none of this. I had no gift, no intuition aiding me all this time. There was nothing more to life other than the mere fact of my physical existence. The divinities I had experienced had been disproved, attributed to a misfiring in my brain, with the same hallucinogenic effect of LSD or opioids. If the door of spiri-tuality, god, the psychic world or whatever, had been slightly ajar until now, then the good folks at 'big pharma' producing my 100mg tablets of lamotrigine had nailed it firmly shut.

Six weeks after his birthday: Cold Case; Soundgarden

Fast forward to six weeks after Richie's birthday and three months since he had gone missing. Smith phoned to say that the case was now officially cold and Richie was being classified as long-term missing. Unofficially, I too had stopped looking for Richie, because I wasn't being paid, and because Quinn had, in no uncertain terms, told me that I needed to focus on rest and recuperation. Which isn't to say he wasn't in my thoughts. He was always there, in the background, as was Kim, Emily, Sophie, and now Francis.

I spent a good chunk of the day deliberating on whether to call Kim. In the end it didn't matter, as she beat me to it. 'I guess you know about Richie.' She was calm, with very little emotion or fight in her words.

'I'm so sorry, Kim. I was sure we were close to finding him.'

'It's okay. In a way we have kind of moved on. I've stopped looking at every forty-something man to see if it's him. It used to be that every time the phone rang or the door chimed, I believed it was Richie. Not now. Even when Detective Smith called, I could tell there was no news.'

'How are the girls?'

'They are handling it well, I think. They don't mention his name much at all. We've adapted to the change. Sometimes it's almost like he never existed for them. It's the trauma though; "they are excising the unwanted from their minds" is what my shrink told me. All part of the healing process.'

'That's good advice,' I lied.

'I didn't thank you for everything you did. But I am now, I guess. You were a comfort.'

She hung up before I could add anything, even if there was little to add. I didn't quite believe that Kim had given up. Or, even if she had said this to others, convinced herself of it, I doubt that she wouldn't still be looking at every white, middle-aged, male stranger's face, looking for his clothes, the blue flanno, the torn jeans, the Temple of the Dog t-shirt, the Converse All-stars. I can't imagine she would feel the same if he were one of her children. I think of the case of Madeline McCann, a name and image that millions of people around the world have heard and seen. Born 12 May 2003; disappeared 3 May 2007. It is in May, every year since, or when new evidence, new leads, are found, that we see renewed calls for information from the public. They show the 'last seen' photo, and they show computer-generated photos and forensic artists' impressions of what she would look like now; her parents (aging in real time) are pleading on TV for her safe return. Do they still look at every little blonde-haired girl, as she was when they last saw her – 90-centimetres tall, her left eye blue and green, her right eye green with a brown spot on the iris – to see if it is their daughter? Or do they draw on the computer-imaging, project into the future, look at every blonde, late-teen girl to see if it is her, frustrated that it is considered impolite to walk up to strangers, right up close, face to face, eye to eye, to see if they match their daughter's. They continue to look for Madeline because she still has two dates that define her – her date of birth and the date of when she went missing. The latter, however, is only a place holder, expedient, an imposter for the second, true, defining, determining date of our lives – the date of our death – which, for both Madeline and Richie, remains, possibly forever, a question mark.

I felt numb after the phone call, at a loose end. The story of Richie, which had so intertwined with my own over the past several months, had come to no real ending, no proper conclusion. The McCann family would be looking for Maddy until the day they die. This is their curse. Kim, however, was already closing the book, unwilling to deal with the absurd project of pursuing something that will likely never come. She was moving on, leaving the past behind as if it were nothing. There is strength in forgetting.

It's hard to describe the following few days other than a state of depression. I didn't leave the house unless absolutely necessary, let my phone go to voicemail, left texts unanswered, avoided all social media. Which didn't go unnoticed by Quinn. And either out of wilful ignorance or her keen penchant for irony, she suggested that I cheer myself up by going to a tribute show for the anniversary of Chris Cornell's death. It was at the Newport in Fremantle, with the cover band playing the whole of Soundgarden's *Superunknown* plus a few songs from their other albums as an encore.

'You like Soundgarden, don't you? I've seen some of their CDs near the stereo. And you had clicked that you were "interested" on the Facebook ad which then popped up on my feed.'

'I'd forgotten about that. But, what about my leg. I can't go to a concert on crutches. And parking in Fremantle is an absolute nightmare – I'd have to take the train with the drunken riff raff.'

'You're just making up excuses. You are getting much sturdier on your crutches and you can have some Panadol before you leave if you're worried about the pain. And I'm sure there will be somewhere to rest it. And I will drive you, Maynard and I, and you *will* have a great time.'

I relented and bought a ticket to the show online – Friday week – but was still making excuses right up to the day and even the hour before we were to leave. 'I shouldn't go. Maynard is a bit sniffly, and his temperature is up.'

'I can handle it. I am capable.'

'How about I stay in so that Maynard and I can watch *Star Wars* – the first one, the original. I've been wanting to do that for ages.'

This didn't appeal to Quinn at all, knowing I, like the other nerds of my generation, would spend most of the time pontificating about how Lucas and co. completely screwed up the original trilogy's legacy with his prequels and sequels.

'We already have our night planned,' she said somewhat sternly, somewhat snootily, like she were invoking Mary Poppins. 'We are dropping you off and getting McDonalds – Maynard's choice – followed by *Jurassic Park*. And that is that.'

It seemed I really had no choice.

As I was driven down Stirling highway, the main artery feeding the Golden Triangle of the Western Suburbs, to a Chris Cornell tribute show, I couldn't help think that if there were any reason for Richie to resurface, make an unexpected public appearance, then this would be the time and place. If he were still in the city, still alive, then why not come and hear the next best thing to one of your favourite bands, if only as a reincarnation. Which for some of us is all we might ever have – a cover band's reincarnation of the bands we loved. And it was luck and chance at the heart of seeing any of those grunge bands live, with such brief windows before the original line-ups collapsed. I was unlucky in never seeing Nirvana, never seeing Alice in Chains with Layne Staley. But I was lucky to have seen Pearl Jam in 1995, and Soundgarden in 1997 following the release of *Down on the Upside* – the album they made before they broke up later that year. I was 19 and it was at the Superdome, near the casino. They began with 'Spoonman' and the crowd went berserk. We surged towards the stage, and the heat rose life a furnace, with sweating bare-chested bodies, t-shirts discarded, already soaked through from the moshpit for You am I – the support act that came before them. We were a tide of bodies, washing towards the breakwall of the stage and then back, with no floor to stand on, only feet and ankles, as you were assaulted by the frenzy: kicked in the shins, kicked in the face by crowd surfers, headbutted. There were bloody noses, and fans passing out from heat exhaustion, crushed on the front fence, dragged over the front fence by nonplussed security. But every one of us, all of us, were grinning, in pained ecstasy, dying on our feet. The only relief from the mayhem was to find your way above the crowd, crowd surf. I pushed myself up, aided, held aloft by the heads, hands, and shoulders of others, my arms spread (not quite a Jesus Christ pose), on my back, sucking in the loud cool air, the music no longer absorbed by the dulling flesh of the crowd, and whose eyes were staring up at me, above them, floating, and then the sudden plummet, falling between the shifting sea to the hard, sticky floor where I was stomped on, kicked, crushed, collapsed on to, panicking at the idea of a suffocating, dark and claustrophobic death. But then hands grabbed me, pulled me up, saved from certain asphyxia by the same humanity that had trampled me.

We were a different crowd for this almost 30-year Soundgarden reunion. Now, it would be social suicide to mosh or crowd surf, and the litigiousness of the twenty-first century curtailed any thoughts of it anyway. And I would be too worried about losing my phone (brand new, iPhone, on a two-year plan), or my wallet which had photos of Maynard and Quinn, and my credit cards, a nearly-complete Perk loyalty card, and barcodes for cheap fuel. I already patted myself down regularly before leaving the house, getting in and out of the car, so any jumping or horizontal movement of my body would be added worry. As a teenager at a concert, my primary concerns would have been for my driver's license to get me into the pubs, and the integrity of a sad unused condom in my pocket, which at the beginning of the night was still hermetically sealed in shiny-optimistic foil, but by the end would have been split and leaking lubricant through my Desert Storm cargo shorts.

It was for these reasons, and my leg, that I stood close to the back, keeping out of others' way, and where I could watch the door and scour the audience, to see if Richie was there. I looked at every face, every shape. Most were around my age and some that were older. More men than women. Like me, many were on their own, balding, overweight. Unrecognisable, dressed like affluent imitations of their former selves. Out of respect for the occasion, I wore a black t-shirt, black jeans, my black Doc Martins, similar to the maroon ones Chris Cornell wore in Soundgarden's early Motorvision video tape. There were younger people too which produced in me mixed feelings: on the one hand I was feeling snobbish, clicked my tongue, condemning them as Johnny-come-latelys, for not being true fans, not like us who were *there* when the band was in its prime, acting like we had discovered them playing those small clubs in Seattle before they got big. On the other, I was heartened, made prideful by the younglings' appreciation of the exquisiteness of Soundgarden, the evidence of the band's generational transcendence and perpetuity that only the greats can achieve.

The cover band took to the stage, barely in their mid-twenties themselves, just babies when Soundgarden were in the throes of dissolving. They should have been nervous, knowing that the older members of the crowd had memorised every chord, every drum roll, every lyric of the album, and even knew the usually-imperceptible mistakes made on the album (I am thinking of Matt Cameron's accidental high hat in the intro of song 15 'Like Suicide'). But this little group were also desperate for any opportunity to hear these songs live again, regardless of whether they were impersonations or not, and so the crowd cheered and clapped enthusiastically and raucously and sincerely. True believers, all of us.

They began, as expected, with 'Let me Drown,' the first song from *Superunknown.*

Again, we cheered, collectively, as the wall of sound consumed us. Should I be wearing earplugs, I asked myself. It was the Berlin Wall all over.

Behind the band, a montage of images from Soundgarden's album covers and music videos were being projected onto the rear stage wall. But I kept watching faces. Some were nodding their heads, some were swaying, others air-drumming, many of them singing along. The majority looked happy, enjoying themselves; some were even laughing with each other, sharing a joke, looking at videos or pictures on their phones. Which is when I started to realise that something didn't feel right. This mood, this revelling in the music, was all wrong. All I could think was: Why are we happy? We shouldn't be happy. Not just because it was a wake of sorts for Chris Cornell, and we should be mournful, respectful of the dead, but because the *Superunknown* playlist was so overtly depressing: 'Let me Drown', 'Fell on Black Days', 'Just like Suicide', 'Limo Wreck',

'The day I tried to live', 'Black Hole Sun.' Death, apocalypse, apathy, suicide, martyrdom. And we were . . . smiling. I wondered, if Chris were still alive, would we be even more joyous? We shouldn't be. It was wrong. If music determined our mood, then it had failed. Or we have failed.

I looked around again, at faces, wanting to communicate my disappointment, to tell them that we were all traitors. That we – the 90's teens, grunge generation, Generation X – had abandoned our essence: our sense of disenfranchisement, our depression, our anger. Betrayed the cause and betrayed ourselves by living successful, well-adjusted, meaningful lives. Betrayed the past by being happy. This was our reunion, and yet there were so few of us. Is this what Richie had felt? Self-deception, duplicity. Someone needed to go backstage and pull the plug, but, before that, snatch away the microphone and scream at them: Have you all forgotten who you are? Don't you remember? Someone needed to tell them what they have done. Not me – I lacked the courage. If only Richie was here. Richie would call us out for what we had become. He knew all along.

I was ready to phone Quinn, ask her to pick me up early with my nose all out of joint. I would have to lie, blame my leg, or maybe dinner wasn't sitting right, or maybe I wanted to watch *Jurassic Park* with Maynard for the first time, to hold his hand during the scary bits with the raptors. She would surely sniff it out though, so I stayed, and when the show ended, I applauded the band, along with the rest, for their technical proficiency and the close-enough imitation of Chris Cornell's voice; for any criticism, any failure of the night's success, lay not with them but with us, their audience. And when the lights came up and we looked around at each other, in a stupor, ears ringing, I looked into the crowd's eyes, their tired old faces, mirrors of my own, and we would have seen each other's disgust and guilt, hidden behind facile middle-class contentment.

I looked, also, one last time, for Richie amongst the faces. But Richie wasn't one of them. And all I could think of as Quinn drove me home, back up the Stirling highway, was that if Richie wasn't there, then he was nowhere.

It was with this understanding that I decided it was time to finally let the case go. It was time to get on with my life, return to the inner sanctum of my family. Maynard was getting older, and would soon be able to manage little tasks of his own, and he could start to go to after-school care a few days a week, make friends, have more playdates. And I would soon need to consider what I was going to do with myself. Quinn had suggested I put my psych skills to new use, specialise in something, upskill. In the meantime, I could start helping out reception at the clinic. She could also pull back a little, start spending more time with Maynard, pick up where she felt she'd left off.

And that's what we did, found balance, structure. There was still my rehabilitation for my leg which included regular visits to the physio and learning again to walk. Which meant I could exercise some more and over the next few months I became fitter than I had been in a long time, not since the academy. I was eating well, fixing up little things around the house, mowing the lawn on Sundays, cheering Maynard on from the sidelines on Saturday-morning soccer. I binge-watched *Twin Peaks*, considered yoga, learned how to bake my own bread, and found instructions on how to make environmentally-friendly cleaners to eradicate the soap scum in the shower.

In the middle of this hive of activity was my own fortieth birthday. With the leg, the diagnosis, all of it, there was little in the way of expectation. It came and went without fanfare. The day after was exactly the same as the day before. No need to run. No need to run and hide. Just find that evenness, balance, structure. Just be.

Eleven months after his birthday

We had our new, calm, and easy routine almost perfected on a Saturday night at home, eleven months after Richie's birthday. We were building a cushion fort for Maynard, had settled on *The Lego Movie* for the night, and an overflowing bowl of microwave popcorn had just been nuked.

'Start it up, Daddy,' plead Maynard, who was near ready to wrestle the remote from my hands.

'Mummy isn't ready yet. Let me just have a quick look at the news headlines.' The first was a breaking story: 'The body of an unidentified man . . .'

'Blah blah blah – Maynard shouldn't watch this – blah blah blah,' Quinn said, coming in from the kitchen, speaking loud over the details.

'Yeah, nah. Let's watch the movie, eh?'

I started it up and hardly gave the headline another thought, until early the following morning when Smith called me, and not for a friendly chat. 'Did you hear?'

'What do you mean?'

'They found a body. Washed up on Heirisson Island, near the Causeway. Male, Caucasian, approximately 40-years old. The press don't have a name yet. But the morgue confirmed it was Richie.'

'They're sure it was him?' I asked, because that's what everyone asks when you're not ready to hear something.

'Yeah, it's him.' The defeat in Smith's voice confirmed the truth.

'What was the cause of death?'

'Still waiting on the full autopsy. Likely it was a heroin overdose, but could have been by drowning. Apparently, he was naked except for a belt around his arm. He was also extremely underweight, probably been living on the streets for a while.'

If I was asked, I would say that I was shocked by the news, and saddened for his daughters who will no longer have their father in their lives. Or that I was relieved, for Kim and myself, our search being over, now able to move on, earnestly, if it were possible. That's what I would say if I was asked. But that wasn't what I was feeling. No, from somewhere, deep, deep, deep within the grey coral folds of my hippocampus (via the temporal lobe), beneath the normal and healthy emotions of a well-adjusted, law-abiding, two-fruit-and-three-veg family man, was instead a dull flicker of . . . admiration; a warm appreciation for his conviction, his commitment to our little group right up until the end. Richie was never missing; he was never a betrayer, either. Just the opposite. He'd found himself, and stayed true to the repressed ghost of our generation. He was who we were. Which I admired.

'Have you told Kim?'

'Yes, she knows.'

A few hours after Smith's call. The sun was bright through hailing leaves – Autumn again – as I drove through western suburb streets. Men were mowing lawns, kids were jumping on trampolines, older couples were walking old dogs. If it wasn't for the dead body of Richie found in the river, and an ambiguous weight on my conscience, then there could be very few explanations for finding myself in Kim's neighbourhood.

When I turned on to her street, I found cars parked all the way up and down, making it almost too narrow to drive through. My first thought was that the word had gotten out, and friends and family had come to console them. But as I drove past their home,

I saw that, instead of a gathering of mourners, they were having a garage sale. Kim was outside, with her two daughters, and they were talking to friends and neighbours and customers. The girls were pointing at things, showing them, helping their mother.

I parked up the road, and discreetly entered through the white-picket gate, instead of the driveway, which was furnished with folding tables, displaying the items for sale. Kim didn't recognise me when I approached her. She was in salesperson mode, all business, dressed accordingly, practically, leggings, singlet, pony-tail, bum-bag holding a float of loose change. When she did see me, she smiled warmly, offered me a hug with air kisses on the cheek, like old friends that hadn't brunched in a while.

'Welcome to our garage sale! See anything you like?'

'I'm not quite sure yet,' I said, playing along. 'You're moving?'

'Gosh, no. Just a clean out. Making some space.'

I looked past her, unintentionally, at their big five-bedroom house, the empty open garage, before again scanning the items for sale: fishing rods, old bikes, and some familiar items: CDs, video consoles, and several boxes labelled 'urns.' All of it was Richie's.

Kim watched me as I attempted to come to an understanding of what was happening here. She came clean, addressing the Richie-shaped elephant in the room. 'Detective Smith called me this morning. I know what you're thinking: it's not a good look, like I didn't care about him or that I didn't love him. That's not true at all. I loved him. The girls loved him. But we needed to get our lives back. It sounds cold, but it felt like he was gone long before today and long before he went missing. Smith told me about the drugs, too. That wasn't the final straw, but let's say it was a convenient justification for how I felt. Anyway, this garage sale was planned weeks ago. You can check my Facebook page and the local papers if you don't believe me.'

'That does explain the big turnout,' I conceded, and looked around at the many milling bargain hunters.

'I know, it's great, isn't it.' Kim was pleased with herself. More than I had noticed before, she used her hands as she spoke, gesturing excitedly, unencumbered, and not just for waving to more familiar faces as they came. That is, until she again remembered why I was there, and adjusted herself accordingly. 'We also need the money for legal bills. They're still chasing us. And Richie's death won't stop them either. Please don't tell the girls, not yet.'

'I won't.'

'Thank you. Now, instead of making them suspicious of why you *are* here, how about you put on a smile and pick something out that you like – mates' rates.'

I didn't feel good about pawing through a dead man's things. The spirit of his being not yet cold, even if his body was. Still, I put on a smile as instructed and started ambling through the rows, wondering if everyone there had engaged in some mass delusion, where they live in a world where Richie has been erased, had never existed, written out of his own history. But everything there – things and objects, the objectively and subjectively valuable – were all inscribed with Richie. This was his archive on display, laid bare, marked with hand-written price tags, sold to strangers, dispersed, scattered indifferently, like a murderer's ashes.

Saddened, I made to leave until, out of the corner of my eye, I spotted the lithograph of Munch's 'The Scream,' the one from their living room, now propped up against the wall, near a leaking hose and with the sun streaming onto it. I picked it up, rescued it, and held it up to Kim. 'How much for this?'

She screwed-up her face. 'Ugh. It's yours. I always hated it. It depressed me every time I came home and the colours clashed with every bit of furniture in the house. Please, take it. *Gratis*.' Kim then shooed it away theatrically and laughed attractively.

'The Scream' is hung in my study, which, since leaving the hospital, is where I have been writing Richie's story. It hangs on the opposite wall to my caricature of Sartre. They complement each other, mirrors of sorts, because of their belonging to the broad existential oeuvre. Munch described the inspiration of 'The Scream' as coming from a walk on a road with two friends; he stopped and stood, trembling with anxiety, sensing an infinite scream passing through nature. Later interpretations suggest it is a painting of existential angst, the anxiety of the human condition, of our finitude. At least this is what Wikipedia tells me. Sartre, opposite, eschewing the mystery of symbolism, proclaimed that 'existence precedes essence,' and that 'man is condemned to choose.'

Sartre is as much to blame as anyone for setting me on this path, as it was Sartre that introduced me to the existential paradox that afflicts my clients. They want to go back to a time in their past, to a certain age, and they want to stand in that same place. But we can't walk in our own old shoes. This past does not exist. It is nothingness. Our being once occupied a certain space, shaped like our body, at a certain time. The body continues on, as does time and consciousness, but the space that was occupied no longer exists.

Just yesterday, I would find myself occupying a certain time and space, maybe at Kim's garage sale, or on the carpet playing Lego. There would be memories of it, maybe even photos, but it does not exist as I exist right now, present, at my desk in my study, and I cannot return to it. Tomorrow, I cannot return to this present moment. If I could, I would find my yesterday-self sitting in my chair, the two of us arguing over the rightful ownership of the same space – the original, present self of yesterday, believes he is deserving because of his innate, hard-wired desire to exist; the time-traveller from the future present, however, superior with wisdom, chastises the past self for their ignorance and lack of appreciation for what he has, and thus declares himself the rightful owner and orders the past self to kindly get out of his fucking chair.

This is why I can say that, as much as they complement each other, Sartre and Munch antagonise each other too from across the room. For Sartre, the past does not exist and is powerless to determine our present and future selves. But 'The Scream', I believe, is our selves screaming from the past, a silent scream. The scream is beckoned by the déjà vu – the moment that our past and present selves come together – and is a scream which has happened before or is about to happen, but never comes or has already been. The scream is frozen; it is the past wanting to reclaim its existence to which it has become a nothingness. It is also our future selves wanting to scream at our present selves to treasure that existence. Not in photos, videos, not even in memories. So that we may never go missing again.

The funeral for Richie came a week later. I attended, hanging at the back. I watched Kim and her daughters follow the hearse, and the simple casket within, as it made its way to the chapel. They each concentrated on their steps and grief, and whether genuine or no, at times looked closer to a rehearsed performance for the mourning audience. From the chapel's speakers came Temple of the Dog's 'Say Hello to Heaven.' Only the attuned would have recognised it, its faint murmur, but it was unmistakeable when Chris Cornell's high vocals soared above the babble of the full house, at least a hundred people, more, all coming from Richie's various lives. Richie died young which meant that most of those who knew him were also those that had survived him. And all I could think of was that, just as much as I was afraid of dying too early, I was equally afraid of dying old, of living to see all my friends and family pass away, one after another, and taking with them their memoires of who I was. Better to die young and live in the memories of the living, keeping you alive until the last of them are gone. So that they can tell your story, of when you were young and beautiful, and wrote love letters and felt free, and romanticised the future. So that others will know that you weren't always that last self – the junkie, the palliated, the has-been.

Both Stevo and Trev were there, as was a sheepish Austin, with Jamie beside him, keeping up appearances. Tommy Clayton was there too, and sat only a row behind Kim and the girls. Damien was one of the apologies read out, as was Richie's father who was too ill to leave the home. I didn't think Debbie and Francis were there but I spotted them waiting at the back, on the opposite side to me. They looked equally saddened and uncomfortable, as if they were strangers amongst the mourners, having accidentally walked into the wrong funeral. Now was not the time to reveal an illegitimate child. Maybe when the ash settles.

Kim gave the eulogy, flanked by her daughters, who rubbed their mother's back as she spoke of Richie's past, whilst a montage of photos played on a screen behind them – the same photos that I ordered against my CDs nearly a year ago. His life, forty years, condensed into a five-minute runtime, before replaying itself, doing it all again, the man at his end returning to his youth. Kim, dry-eyed, spoke of his life as a timeline, focussing on dates and places; and in doing so enabled Richie to escape being defined by what they knew of him, which seemed to be very little. It also seemed that no goals remained unfilled by his life being cut short. He was complete, whole. And without legacy, except on his daughters' faces: Richie's lips and chin, which trembled achingly, and ran wet with tears from their mother's eyes.

I decided not to stay for the wake because I could feel the eyes of the mourners on me, the word getting around that I was the detective Kim had hired to look for him. They wanted to know if I could solve the mystery for them. They wanted to know if I'd found his 'Rosebud', so that they could attach some meaning to the man they thought they knew. There was no mystery, and, although I had no physical evidence, I did know his Rosebud: a syringe, a black-burnt crucible spoon, lighter, a thumbnail of brown sugar heroin wrapped in foil. These were the objects, the things, essences I should have been looking for all along.

This is why I didn't hang around for the wake. And, besides, I had to collect Maynard from school. I waited with the other parents; we talked about our children. I asked mistakenly about how their weekends were when it was already closer to the next. I was excused when the siren rang, and, like a burst weir, our children exited the classroom. The throng steadily fanned out, and, like flotsam, Maynard floated my way, grinning with anticipation of the modest adventures that awaited him in these after-school hours. When I asked, he told me that school was 'good' and, yes, he ate all of his lunch.

The bones and the scar of my leg had healed and I had been off the crutches for over six months, but I was still hobbled to some degree. I was indignant at the OT's offer of a cane, not wanting to add further affectation or age to my guise; and refused it for Maynard's sake, sparing him the embarrassment of his friends seeing his ailing father. But Maynard was keen to get home and was a dozen steps ahead of me, skipping along. I called out to him: 'Hey slow down a little, will ya! Who do you think you are, Robert de Castella or something?'

He stopped and came back to me, a look on his open face like he had just figured out some very clever and grown-up scheme. He suggested that maybe he could start walking to and from school by himself, counting his reasoning out on his fingers: it wasn't that far; he would be careful when crossing the road; and some kid in his class already was. It seemed his new front teeth, the uniform that almost fit him now, the slightly broader shoulders that his school-bag just hung upon, had afforded him a new sense of confidence and independence.

I was composed, took it in my stride. 'Not yet buddy. Let's wait a little while before we make that leap.'

'Okay,' he said, surprisingly without fuss, and then reached for my hand and interlaced his tiny soft fingers with mine, squeezed them together, tight and tender and warm, bonded by love and blood. As if to say, with the wise ignorance of youth, 'Everything will be alright, Daddy. I promise. Everything will be just fine. Just you wait and see.'

ACKNOWLEDGMENTS

I would like to again thank my beautiful partner Melanie and my darling son for their patience and support for my writing. Thank you also to my mum and dad and brother for their encouragement. And thank you to my writing friends, Brooke Dunnell, Kevin Price, Wendy Glassby and Michelle Michau-Crawford, as well as Dr Rashida Murphy for her fantastic insights and suggestions.

www.ingramcontent.com/pod-product-compliance
Lightning Source LLC
Chambersburg PA
CBHW030629120726
47904CB00006B/2083